NORTH
ON THE
YELLOWHEAD

And Other Crime Stories

DONNA CARRICK

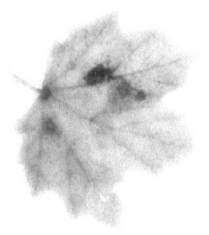

North on the Yellowhead

and Other Crime Stories

Donna Carrick

Print Edition 2016
ISBN 13: 978-1-77242-050-0

Carrick Publishing

Print Edition, License Notes:

Table of Contents

Praise for *The First Excellence*

*Winner of the 2011 Indie Book Event Award fo
r excellence in fiction.*
~ The Indie Book Collective, July, 2011

*Top Read for 2010! Donna Carrick has what should be,
and hopefully WILL become, a best seller.*
~ The Sunday Book Review

*An exquisitely-crafted saga of one person's search for her roots set
against a clash of cultures. An intricate plot that mirrors the subtlety of
China itself…*
~ Jim Napier, The Sherbrooke Record, February 18, 2011,
also Deadly Diversions

*…compelling storylines…A complex mystery with multiple plots and a
host of intriguing characters. …pleasantly unpredictable…*
~ Kirkus Discoveries

I highly recommend this book, read it, you won't be disappointed.
~ Barbara Kent, Success Books

*I fell in love with this book from the first two paragraphs. It grabs your
attention and doesn't let go until well after you finish…* ~ The Book
Journal

Other Titles

The First Excellence, ©2009/2011

Gold And Fishes, ©2006/2011

The Noon God, ©2006/2011

Sept-Îles and other places, ©2011

Knowing Penelope, ©2012

Thanks as always to my husband, Alex, and to our children.

See how he turns, stops and then sighs…
In the darkness he dies
For the taste of one beautiful word:
Mercy.

~ *Donna Carrick*

NORTH ON THE YELLOWHEAD

It's not much farther, I tell myself. My eyes are bleary with prairie fatigue and my mind is a slide show of wheat fields and grain elevators. It's been so long. I'd almost forgotten how it feels to see the sky stretching out all around me. Almost....

There it is — the town where I grew up; the bank where I deposit my earliest memories; the place that broke my heart even as it breathed life into my spirit.

That dot on the map, north of Yorkton on the Yellowhead Highway.

First stop, the town's cenotaph. That's where the memories begin and end, at the monument dedicated to those who died in both of the great wars. I park my car on the road that is now paved – though in my memory it will always be carved in dirt, the hot dust rising in the unforgiving afternoon.

This is where he died. Or, so I am told, this is where his body was found a week ago, on a cool October morning. It was foul play, the paper said. Nothing fancy ... a blunt instrument to the back of the head.

I got the call from an old friend. *I thought you'd like to know... Lester LeBlanc... Dead.* Yeah. I guess I'd like to know.

I remember Lester — tall, dark, painfully young, a serious Metis teenager with a saxophone under his arm, black eyes flashing behind thick glasses, a smile always lurking at the corner of his mouth, but never quite coming into flower.

I remember the early days of spring, when I was thirteen, before I knew for certain the world was really as hard a place as it seemed to be — the little white church nestled in a profusion of lilac and honeysuckle, the grounds a forest of color filled with sweetly scented air.

Lester started coming to our church in the spring of that year. He came alone. His family were not church-going people. He came because the minister told him he could play his saxophone for the congregation every Sunday morning. The things a clergyman will do to save a soul....

He was fifteen that year, a stringy colt of a boy standing alone before the all-white congregation. Just a boy and his horn. Then he raised it to his mouth and he was instantly transformed, no longer merely a gangly, self-conscious, pimple-peppered kid. The music rose and fell with a sacrilegious beauty, lifting Lester up to the status of a god, and lifting me, the untried spirit, into the clouds.

Until that day, music had been something one had to endure, a part of the noise of daily living — the sorry twang of the country radio, and *Did your chewing gum lose its flavor on the bedpost overnight?*— the crow-like offering of the townsfolk, *Oh, come, come, come to the church in the wild wood....*

That day my ears were opened with a heavenly flood of sound, cascading through the undiscovered regions of my brain, charting new synapses with each impassioned sliding of the scale.

Oh, beautiful boy, to stand before us mortals creating such a sound.

"That was nice," I said on the steps of the church after the service.

"Thanks. Wanna go for a walk?"

And so we became Sunday afternoon sweethearts, meeting out of sight of the elders after all the singing and the praying were done, holding hands under the lilac trees and kissing behind the church in the heavy bush.

Of course, we knew we'd better not get caught. Nice white girls didn't mess around with Métis country boys. It wouldn't go well for either of us.

Lester lived near Good Spirit Lake, on a small farm with his father and uncle. He had a twin brother whose name I can't remember, and a younger sister, about my age. I think she had a learning disability. She went to school on a nearby Reservation.

We didn't talk much, Lester and me. But every Sunday I'd be there with bells on at the church, waiting for the music that would free my soul.

And every Sunday after church we'd come together, our mouths growing familiar with each other and our hands searching for something we couldn't name.

I shield my eyes and peer down the street to the right of the cenotaph, towards the brick schoolhouse where I first met Lester. Grades one through six, all housed in a four-room building, two classrooms on the main floor and two upstairs. A seesaw, a set of swings, and a Giant Strides, now defunct thanks to too many broken legs and too many lost teeth.

I didn't know him then, really. He was one of a pair of twins, two years older than I was. By the time I was in grade six he had moved on to Junior High in Yorkton. A year later his brother died — a tragic accident involving a train.

We were all fascinated by the prairie trains, with their speed and fury. Walking along the tracks in search of tiger lilies was a favorite pastime among the young people. From time to time you'd hear of some kid getting ripped apart by one of the great metal monsters. In fact, I'd even known one girl who'd chosen 'death by train' as a form of suicide.

I know I'm going to wander around the school grounds, peer into the windows and sit in the dust on the baseball diamond. But I'll wait till later in the afternoon, after school is out.

For the moment I am expected down the road, at the General Store, that is, at one of two competing General

Stores that still stand stubbornly across the main street from each other, as if this one-horse town could ever hope to support two stores. Paulette Snow now runs Snow's Store since her father passed away. When she called to tell me about Lester she offered to let me stay at her place while I was in town.

I hear the soft jangling of the bell as the door swings open. The Mars Bars and the M & M's make me smile. It's good to know I haven't really walked straight into the past — that even here, in this bastion of antiquity, something of the new millennium has ventured. When I was a kid drooling over this counter it was all Smarties and Popeye Candied Cigarettes. Big black Jawbreakers...

Paulette hears the bell and emerges from the back room, looking like nothing has changed since the last time we saw each other. She was beautiful then, and she is still beautiful, dressed in the latest fashion, looking like one of Charlie's Angels. Her hair is longer than it was when she married the Mayor. Oh, yeah, her name is different now. Paulette MacNeil.

She was a lovely bride. Her mother, president of the local Four-H Club, created her dress of the finest silk, shipped in especially from Montreal. Her golden curls escaped from her frothy veil, framing her heart-shaped face with its pouting mouth.

"Come in, stranger," she says, her face beaming.

The memories overwhelm me. I remember that day, when my family first set foot in this town. We were supposed to move to the nearby Air Force base, but my father wanted to stop to ask directions, so he pulled off the highway and parked outside of Snow's store. He liked the town, so we stayed.

Paulette once confided to me her memory of that day.

"I thought you were the weirdest thing on two feet," she laughed. "You were all dressed up for the Wild West, in your cowboy hat and boots. Big City tenderfoot heading for the badlands."

Her easy laughter still hurts. Even when we were only eight I knew Paulette was special. She was the town's golden child, in her dainty patent shoes with her curls all bound in pink ribbons. My memory of that day was different from hers. In my version we became instant friends.

"How's it going?" I ask, following her into the house built onto the back of the store. Paulette doesn't live there anymore, of course. She and Mayor Bill MacNeil have a new large house at the other end of Main Street. But Paulette's mother still rattles around in this comfortable cage, sewing fancy dresses for her grandchildren.

"It's going OK," she answers. "Mom's out with Brian for the day." Brian is Paulette's older brother, the artist.

"How is her arthritis?"

"Not bad. Knitting keeps her hands limber." She waves her hand toward the wicker basket beside the rocker where a mountain of pastel-colored yarn sits waiting.

"Have you heard any more about Lester?" I ask. It's been a long drive – all the way from Toronto around the northern tip of Superior, through Kenora and Manitoba.

"The funeral's tomorrow. Bill says they're pretty sure Shelly had something to do with it, but there's no evidence."

I close my eyes, watching the rings that float behind my lids, warmed by the stream of light that pours in through the homemade lace curtains. *Shelly Gogaletz. Shelly Gogaletz LeBlanc.* The name still howls like a freight train in my ears.

I remember Shelly. She was fifteen the year I was thirteen, the wayward daughter of elderly Ukrainian farmers, growing up as wild as thistle on a prairie lawn. Her hair fell long and brown down to her waist, and her blue eyes flashed a willful green in the sunlight. She wore her tube top high and her hipsters low, a yellow happy face stitched onto the back pocket of her hash jeans. She knew how to work a smile.

But I was just jealous. We all wore our hipsters low that year. Shelly simply wore them better than the rest of us, her reed-like trunk swaying naked as she moved, her laughter loud and ready.

"I liked your last C.D.," Paulette says, moving toward the rack. "Do you mind if I play it?"

"Not at all. Thanks." I've been taking lessons in good grace from my sister. Tillie says I don't know how to deal with my success. She says I tend to wave away compliments, and my doing so is vaguely rude, as if my fans should find more productive ways to spend their time, rather than listening to my music.

She's right, of course, so I'm trying to be more gracious. Trying to enjoy the fact people buy my CDs of their own free will.

I never expected success — never willed it to come to me. It was just a by-product of the music. I've been blessed with a love so deep it can only be called corny, a love so real it can't be measured in terms of the mundane. Success came as a result of that love. I'm still not wholly comfortable with it.

Two husbands came and went, the first a flash of fury, howling through the night, the second, gentle lover that he was, dead these past three years. No children. My parents long gone, mother to cancer and father to a broken heart. My sister so much younger than me even our mutual love sometimes cannot climb the wall of our separate upbringings. My own childhood wrapped and tucked away like an unwanted present in a dusty corner of the prairies, twenty miles north of Yorkton on the Yellowhead Highway.

And me, alone, for the most part, in Toronto, surrounded daily by producers and agents and media. Singing and playing to an almost empty room, to a lone ghost sitting in the corner, to the one who first brought me this love of music: Lester LeBlanc.

But now Lester is gone, too, and my memories come crashing down around my ears, faster than I can hope to gather up the pieces.

Shelly. Damn her. Damn her blue-and-sometimes-green reckless, fickle eyes!

"Did anyone see him that night?" I ask, afraid of the answer. I've been afraid ever since I started on this quest someone is going to tell me a truth I would rather not hear about Lester. About his death, and more importantly, about his life.

The last I'd heard he and Shelly had moved into his father's farmhouse. They had three kids and two dogs. No one had heard him play the saxophone in years, not since his father died. His uncle moved into a nursing home, but his sister still lived on the farm with Lester and Shelly. At least that's what I heard.

"Arnold saw him at the hotel," Paulette says. The 'hotel' is a four-room inn with a bar attached to it, a dingy hole where the local men gather to drink beer and shoot the shit.

"Who was he with?"

"A couple of guys. A white guy and a Métis. Arnold says he saw the Métis once or twice before with Lester."

"Have they come forward?" I ask.

"Not yet. But Bill says they've got notices out everywhere. Meanwhile Shelly's doing her 'speak-no-evil' dance all over the cops. They can't get anything out of her."

"She hasn't changed?"

"Not a bit. Still living hard and fast. Haven't seen her sober in years."

"Still gets around?"

"Yeah. Rumor was she was messing with Lester's uncle before they put him in a home. Poor old guy was in his seventies. Must've thought he'd died and gone to heaven the day she moved in."

"She never should've married."

"She never should've had three kids, either, but she did, her and Lester. Hell of a life, having a mother like that. Knowing everyone is talking behind her back, and their father more a shadow than a man."

What was he like, I wondered, *as a man?* I only knew the boy, the sweet, hot lover who lay beside me in the cool grass under the lilac trees. The child who pulled the honeysuckle flowers from the branches so we could sip their nectar. I remembered the way he smelled, the way he tasted, the way his hands felt on my half-developed woman's body.

The promise of it all, the expectations. Gone forever in a single season.

We kissed and touched and rubbed our growing bodies together, our desire mounting with each passing Sunday afternoon. All through the summer we continued, frightened and exalted by the music we were making. Sweet virgin youth, awkward and bold, excruciatingly ardent.

"Have you eaten?" Paulette asks, shattering my reverie, and my stomach growls, despite my need for sleep.

"Not since breakfast."

We walk three blocks north toward the Yellowhead Grill, now called the Prairie House Grill, according to the sign, which is badly worn by at least a dozen relentless winters. I don't care. To me it will always be the Yellowhead Grill, the place where my friends and I met for endless cokes and hamburgers.

I recognize her right away, although I don't know the man she is with. Caroline Bigelow, at one time the prettiest girl in town. All the boys were crazy about her.

Forty seems to have hit her like a fist full of frump, although her eyes are still alive with humor. In fact, she looks just like her mother, the merry-eyed, jowly piano teacher who played the organ every Sunday at our church.

She looks at me, then looks away, then sees Paulette beside me and puts two and two together.

"Hi," she says, her cherubic face lighting up. "I heard you were coming. Just can't stay away, can you?"

The jibe isn't lost on me. Since we'd moved away when I was fifteen, I'd been back only twice, once to show off husband number one, who lasted barely three months after our visit, and the second time to stand as Maid of Honor at Paulette's wedding.

In my heart, of course, I'd never left. But Caroline couldn't have known that.

"Hi, Caroline. Good to see you." She stands and I throw my arms around her, suddenly moved by the sight of her. It hits me now, as I allow myself to be drenched in her smile. I'm back. Twenty-five years later, and alone, but still, I'm back.

I push down the emotion and let her go, waiting for the introduction.

"My husband, Sid Sheppard," she says, nodding at the balding country gentleman beside her.

"And of course I know who you are," he says, grinning warmly. "We're your biggest fans. We bought your latest album just last week. *Tears on the Sand.* It's brilliant."

"Thank you," I smile graciously, thinking of Tillie. I wonder what she's doing now, what park bench she is sitting on, under what tree, and whether she is holding her favorite blue fountain pen in one hand and resting her notebook on her knee. My sister the poet, the lost fairy princess, recorder of all things sweet and innocent. Scribbler of refined and delicate thoughts, dreamer of finer dreams than the rest of us will ever know.

He seems like a good man, I think, *even if he isn't much to look at.* Besides, looks are no measure of a man. I recall "husband number one", with his lovely boyish face, his angel blonde hair, and his deadly temper. I wonder, even after all these years, how I managed to escape the terror of those years. Beautiful on the outside, but ugly as death on the inside.

"When did you two tie the knot?" I ask, smiling at Caroline and Sid.

"Just last year," they answer in unison. New love. "We're late bloomers," Sid laughs.

"I waited and waited till I'd almost given up," Caroline says. "Then, when I least expected it, along came Mr. Right."

Paulette and I join them and we order lunch, laughing and sharing anecdotes over sandwiches and coffee ... snatches of stories that are supposed to capture the gist of the years that have passed since we were all children here together in this very diner, on a day not very different from today.

After lunch, Paulette makes her excuses. "Gotta get back to the store," she says. "Wouldn't want to lose any of my rip-roaring business." We all laugh. It's a mystery to me how her family managed to make a living all those years.

"I'm going to stay awhile," I say, "and visit with Caroline. Then I'd like to take a walk. See if I remember any of the old places."

"I guess the town will be crawling with press before we know it," Sid says good-naturedly.

"No," I answer quickly. "No one knows I'm here."

"Don't worry," Caroline laughs. "Your secret's safe with us."

I am relieved.

"I'll see you in a few hours," I say, waving to Paulette as she leaves the diner. I smile at her smile, and it's like the years never happened.

"What's the occasion?" Caroline asks. "Paulette told me you were coming, but she didn't say why."

"Lester's funeral. Paulette remembered I went to school with him."

"Lester LeBlanc. Yeah. The cops have been hanging around town asking lots of questions. I didn't know you and he were friends."

"Only for a little while," I fudge the truth. "He used to come to our church one summer."

"I remember that. He used to play the Sax — he was pretty good, too. But I don't remember you spending much time with him."

So we'd fooled them all, with our slipping away, meeting in the bushes after everyone was gone. No one had known. It was a secret I had never shared with anyone, not even Tillie.

From late May through early October, our bodies growing more urgent with each meeting. Until the day Lester finally became bold enough to lead me to the haunted house, the old abandoned building next door to the church. We climbed in through a half-boarded window and stretched out on the floor, free at last from the dreadful fear of discovery.

"I love you," he said, pulling me close, his hands lifting my sweater to reveal my breasts.

"I love you," he said, tearing at my jeans and panties so my naked skin was pressed against the cold surface of the dirty floor.

"I love you," he repeated, his penis hard against my thigh, pushing, pushing against me in an undeniable wave of passion.

"I love you, too," I whispered, feeling him slide into me, and feeling the pain that comes from being broken.

It lasted only minutes, and afterwards he held me softly in his arms while I wept, not knowing what it was I was weeping for. He kissed me and helped me with my clothes, and all the while he kept whispering 'I love you' till I couldn't help but believe we were, in fact, in love.

Who knows? Maybe we were.

But shortly after that Lester stopped coming to our church on Sunday and I didn't see much of him around. I heard he was spending time with Shelly Gogaletz, and the green-eyed monster of jealousy swallowed me whole.

Shelly was fifteen, the same age as Lester. Her body put mine to shame, with its maturity. Rumor had it she'd already been around.

By Christmas it was common knowledge Shelly was pregnant. Shotgun weddings were not uncommon in these parts, but this one had the added scandal of being a mixed marriage. I remember her smug satisfaction the day she brought her newborn into the diner, pushing the pram in front of her like it was first prize in the lottery. She smiled an especially demeaning smile at me, and for a chilling moment I thought she must know — Lester must have told her about our love.

But the moment passed, and I realized if she had, in fact, known about Lester and me she would have made a spectacle of herself by starting some ridiculous catfight. She was not a woman who could walk away from the opportunity to flaunt her lack of couth.

"Are you all right?" Caroline asks, reaching for my hand.

"Yeah," I say. "Just a bit tired. It's been a long drive. What were you saying?"

"I was saying I don't remember you being particularly friendly with Lester."

"I guess I wasn't, really. We talked a bit. But I liked him, you know?"

"I understand," she says, still holding my hand. "Besides, it's great to see you again, no matter what the reason."

"Tell me, Caroline," I begin, not sure how to broach the subject, "do you have any idea who would want to hurt Lester? He was an easy-going guy, not the sort of fellow who would make a lot of enemies."

"One of *her* men, most likely," she says, meaning Shelly.

"What would be in it for her?"

"The farm, the house. Not worth much in resale value. But the kids are nearly grown. She could sell it and move into the city."

"What about insurance? Paulette was saying Bill thinks Shelly had something to do with it, but they can't prove it. Would Lester have had life insurance?"

"Probably. But between you and me, Bill's in no position to be digging very deeply."

"Why?"

Caroline shakes her head again, looking at her husband. "I hate to say it," she says, "but everyone around here knows it anyway. Bill's been banging Shelly for years, since long before he and Paulette got married."

"Are you sure?" I am incredulous. The Mayor Bill MacNeil, dipping his wick into one of the most notorious scarlet women ever known to man. To men. To many men. And Paulette must have known. Could she be that obtuse?

"Yeah," Sid agrees. "We're sure. He used to brag about the stuff she'd do for him. He'd have a few beers, then get all randy and let the rest of us know he was gonna pay the great dame a visit. I got the idea he wasn't getting what he needed at home."

"Big surprise there," Caroline says, and I wonder what she means. Then it starts to make sense. Paulette was always more concerned with appearances than with feelings. I wonder what it would be like to be married to her.

I push the thought away, feeling like a traitor. After all, she is my friend.

"How could Lester have put up with Shelly all those years?" I ask the air.

"Cuckold syndrome," Sid says. "Once he started turning a blind eye, it just got easier all the time."

"And then there were the kids," Caroline says. "Someone had to raise them. It sure wasn't gonna be her royal majesty. She was busy doing the town."

Lester, I think, *how did it come to this?* Would it have been different, I wonder, if it had been me? If I had been the one to present him with a swollen belly? Would his life have been better? Would mine?

But bitter irony, the truth, what it took me two marriages to learn, my body was as barren as a prairie winter.

No babies here, no howling brats to disturb your sleep or running noses to break your heart. No chains to bind your love to me faster than a speeding bullet.

Oh, Lester. Where did your music go?

"Do you ever see Dorrie?" I ask, struggling to drag myself back into the present. For that is all there is now, the present, no future anymore, and the past a dust-covered relic in the attic of my mind.

"Yeah. She gets out most days. It's hard since Krishka passed away."

Krishka, Dorrie's mother, was a crazy old Ukrainian woman who never learned a word of English and who roamed the village streets in the morning ranting at the crows. She was famous for her homemade mustard, the best to be had anywhere, and for her pirogues, which she sold door-to-door along with eggs from their near-by chicken farm.

It amazed me that someone like Dorrie could have come from Krishka. Dorrie was the most intelligent person I ever met. The best friend I had ever had, bar none. Always three steps ahead of the rest of us. Always the planner, the one with big dreams.

Dorrie was the valedictorian in her senior year. We lost touch after she married an actor and moved to Regina. I waited for the day when I would hear her first book had been published.

Instead, her marriage ended and she went home to care for her aging mother. But in the later years it was Krishka who had to look after Dorrie.

I know the tears are close at hand, so I excuse myself, leaving the new lovers behind to enjoy another coffee. I have roads to walk upon, memories to spin.

I step into the early afternoon sunlight, not wanting to obscure my vision with sunglasses. Not today. I want to look upon this town as it really is, in all of its drab glory. I want to revel in the half-remembered and the fictional, the truth and the fantasy we call memory.

And so I walk, past the two General Stores that still stand stubbornly across from each other, to the cenotaph where I last saw him on that cold November morning. I was fifteen, and he was seventeen. She wasn't there with him, but he carried his infant son upon his shoulders, proud as ever a father could be. The town elders led the way, carrying the wreath we would place at the base of the monument.

About two hundred townsfolk, a scraggly parade of sorts, marching down the one main street. Most dressed in black, all wearing hats and gloves against the start of winter.

I saw Shelly wasn't with him, so I waved, just to let him know I forgave him, that it was all OK, but he didn't see me, or pretended not to, and I lost him in the sullen throng. I could have forced the issue. Could have looked again and seen the infant high above the other marchers, could have sidled up to him. But to say what? That his son was as beautiful as he was? That I longed to hold him one more time, to be a woman with him?

I didn't lose sight of him that day. I let him go. And now I have to let him go again. That's the reason I'm here.

I tromp around the school ground, sitting on the wooden swings and listening to the ghostly sounds of teachers long dead or retired, chirping orders to unruly farm boys. But the sun is getting low, so I make my way towards the edge of town, to the last lot before the wheat fields begin. It only takes me five minutes to walk the distance, past the tiny post office and the churches, past Janie's house, where we made water bombs from balloons, to the large double lot where I used to live.

They've finally torn it down, that four-room hovel, that house of terror where I suffered seven lonely years of childhood. That eyesore, that monstrosity. I can't blame them. Still, I would have liked to see it one more time, just to try to sort out the real from the imagined in my store of grievances.

Oh, well. Turning away, I walk next door to Dorrie's house. Might as well get it over with.

"How are you?" she asks, fussing with the chairs, trying to position mine so I won't be staring straight into the setting sun.

"I'm fine, Dorrie. And you?"

"Oh, very well, thank you," she says, twisting a dishrag in her hands. "I haven't seen you for a long time. What have you been doing?"

She doesn't know, of course, what I've been doing. She doesn't follow the news, the entertainment scene. To her I'm just an old friend. It might have been a week, a year or twenty years since we last saw each other. It doesn't matter to Dorrie.

"Have some pirogues," she says, slopping the potato-filled dumplings onto a plate. "Mom made them fresh this morning."

"Thank you," I say, taking the greasy dish from her. It doesn't matter that I wouldn't eat them if they came from anyone else. I know I'll eat them all, and I will tell her they are the best things I've had in years.

"Have some homemade mustard with those," she says, spooning a heap of the grainy yellow mixture onto the side.

"Delicious," I mutter between bites.

"Mom made it this summer. I sell it around town. It pays the bills."

"It's good you have an income," I offer lamely.

"Yes, especially since the publisher has been holding back my royalties. I haven't had a check from them in years. The biggest book of the decade, and I haven't seen a penny. Not a penny."

"That's terrible," I agree, aware Dorrie never finished her book. There was no great Canadian novel, no recognition, no success. There were just Dorrie and Krishka, chasing each other through the streets of this town, one as crazy as the other.

And now the ghost of Krishka is busy making pirogues for her daughter.

I hug her and take my leave. I love her – always have – but there's nothing I can do for her.

She understands and walks me to the door.

"Come again," she says, "in another fifteen years. I've missed you."

"I've missed you, too, Dorrie."

There's nothing left to see, and I'm suddenly overwhelmed by an undeniable exhaustion, so I slowly make my way back to Main Street, to Paulette's house at the other end of town.

"Come in," she says. "Supper's ready. Bill's going to be late. They brought someone in on the murder."

She speaks in a hushed tone, like a fellow conspirator, like someone in the know, which, of course, she is.

"This is terrific," I say about the food, ignoring the pile of pirogues that is already hardening in my stomach.

"Thanks," she says. "Can I ask you something?"

"Sure."

"Why didn't you ever tell me about you and Lester?" She is hurt.

"Because," I answer, "I was embarrassed. It was kind of dirty, sneaking off after church to make out with an older boy. And he was Métis. I was worried about my reputation."

She seems satisfied with the lie. It is the kind of rationale she would have applied to the situation. The truth, though, is something a little different.

What I had with Lester was private. It was something I didn't want to share, didn't want to expose to the twittering commentary of my friends. I was afraid if I brought it out into the open I would lose it. Afraid it wouldn't be able to withstand the harsh scrutiny of people like Paulette.

And after I had already lost it, there was the humiliation of it all. It was better dealt with privately.

As we clear the supper dishes, Bill comes bustling in.

"We got the guy," he says, as filled with self-importance as if he was the town Sheriff instead of just the Mayor. As if he'd personally hunted the killer down and dragged him into jail.

"Are you sure it's him?" Paulette asks.

"Yeah. Son of a bitch confessed."

"How did you find him?" I ask.

"The half-breed, Bobby Hogue, came forward. He was out drinking with Lester and Mike Heffernan that night. He said Mike, that's the white guy, told him he was balling Shelly on a regular basis. Mike told him Shelly wanted Lester out of the picture. Had a big insurance policy waiting in the wings."

"Why didn't Bobby stop him?"

"Thought he was all talk. Didn't take him seriously."

"What does Mike say?"

"He says he did it — killed Lester. But he says Shelly had nothing to do with it. He's taking the fall. Thinks he's in love. Poor bastard doesn't know her very well."

I blush for Bill, for what I know about him and Shelly. I blush for Paulette, for what she may or may not know. But neither of them blush. It's all façade to them.

"What time is the funeral?" I ask, yawning. Time to sleep. I need my rest these days, the body breaking down in harmony with the mind.

"Eleven. What time do you want us to wake you?" Paulette asks.

"Don't worry. I don't sleep late." I know I will be up before the sunrise. It is a function of my stage of life — as I fast approach the end, I cling to every moment, wanting to savor it, not wanting to miss a second.

The service is held at our old church. Caroline Bigelow Sheppard plays the organ and the choir sings Amazing Grace. Most of the mourners are curiosity-seekers, out to learn whether I am really in town. The Minister is a young woman whom I have never met. Her voice is pleasing. All in all, it is nicely done.

Paulette suggests I sing a number, but I refuse. I'm not here to showboat. I'm here to say goodbye.

At the moment the congregation rises, though, to form a line to the open casket, I waver in my resolve. I cannot let myself look upon his death. I cannot see what forty-some-odd years of loss and suffering has done to him. At that moment I realize I cannot relinquish my memory of the beautiful, serious boy with the flashing dark eyes and the saxophone under his arm. I opt to keep the memory, and leave the church without that final farewell.

***

"Come again," Paulette says, holding me and dropping a real tear.

"I will," I say, thinking one more lie won't upset the balance of her web of lies.

She helps me carry my bags to the car. The sun is high overhead. When the funeral ended, I realized I just wanted to go home. I wanted to see my sister, Tillie, to let her know she is my home. Wherever she is, my crazy wonderful flower of a sister, that is my home.

"Goodbye, Paulette," I say, "and thanks. Thanks for everything."

"It was nothing," she says, weeping openly now at my leaving. Poor woman. So lonely in her big fine house.

I start to cry as well, and she hugs me.

Before I leave town, though, there is one more stop to make. I couldn't do it at the church, but I have to say goodbye to Lester. I have to tell him I came, let him know I forgive him and I understand.

I hear the gravel crunch under my tires as I pull into the village graveyard. This at least is as I remember it. No pavement here, no trees to block the grueling prairie sun. I find the small stone marker where the dirt is freshly turned and kneel in the thin dusty grass.

"It was a nice service," I say, feeling mildly foolish but determined to talk to him. "I wish you'd been there. You could have played your saxophone. It would have been nice."

I wince, feeling the sharp pain in my breast that comes in spasms now, the inoperable cancer that is blowing like

20

tumbleweed through the badlands of my body. *Live in the moment,* I remind myself. *Don't fear the future. It will play itself out.*

"Maybe I'll see you soon, my friend, on the other side. You never know. Maybe you'll play your saxophone and I'll sing and play my guitar. We were good together."

I stand, shaking the prairie dust from the knees of my trousers. I know I have to get back on the road, before the exhaustion takes hold again. I have to get back to Tillie.

Poor Tillie. What will become of her? Who will save her from the harsh, cold world? I've tried to be some kind of mother to her, as well as a sister, poor motherless Ophelia.

On the way out of town I pause, touching the brake as the tires roll gently over the railroad tracks. I remember the speed and the fury. Maybe it would be a better way to go.

No, I think. It wouldn't do. I have to find it in myself to go with grace, the way Tillie would want me to. The way my mother taught me.

Don't think about the future, I remind myself, picking up speed on the open highway. *There is only now.*

DANCING WITH CAROLE

A statue of the Blessed Virgin graces the highway just outside of town. As children, we seldom paid attention to it. It was just *there*, a part of the landscape we took for granted.

She's a lovely Lady though, standing as She does on the edge of the forest. Her robe is blue and Her head covering is gilded ivory, both of which make striking contrasts against the backdrop of evergreens.

Occasionally we would notice a light in Her halo had burnt out, or someone had left litter at her base. Locals from our town were quick to correct the problem, to change the bulbs or clear the trash, all in honor of Her Holiness.

Once, though, during the infamous FLQ crisis, Our Lady witnessed a rare spot of drama. A local child had gone missing. Her body was found some days later, torn and mangled, abandoned behind Mary's flowing skirts.

According to reports, the abduction was sexually motivated. Our town was especially shocked, given the tender age of the victim. It was not a political crime, but set against the tension of those emotional days, her murder served to heighten local anxiety. We children were warned by parents and teachers not to wander off, and above all, not to talk to strangers.

To see Ste-Marie posed so tenderly, you wouldn't guess She stood guard over more than just trees and sky. Our town is well hidden, marked only by a turning-off from the main road. *Blink*, and you're sure to miss it.

We were a thousand souls at any given count, including a handful of families on surrounding farms who took their mail at our post-office. All Francophone, except for us, and all decidedly R.C.

We were a family of four: Dad, Mom, my younger sister Stephanie, and me, Ruth. I was seventeen at the time, and Stephanie was fifteen.

Our only close neighbors, Carole and Jean-Paul had two preschool children. Jean-Paul would make a rink for them in winter. In summertime our families would sometimes hike together down the dangerous escarpment to the river. When the water was low, the reddish sand would yield clams by the bucketful.

Carole and Jean-Paul were younger than our parents. They couldn't have been more then twenty-five years old. They loved to drive into the city to visit with friends, and often they would ask me to baby-sit. They paid well, and their kids were well-behaved, so I didn't mind. Besides, it was a welcome chance to get out of the house.

It was spring-time, and Carole had asked me over for 5 pm. She and Jean-Paul were meeting friends for dinner, then heading to the town hall for the annual Spring Dance.

They were protective of their little ones, especially after a second child had gone missing earlier that week. Another girl – a six-year-old – had disappeared while walking home from school.

Jean-Paul was late getting home from work, so Carole and I sat together trading stories. She told me about her teen years in an all-girls' Catholic school. She shuddered as she recalled being terrorized by nuns, and laughed in embarrassment at her own naiveté regarding the opposite sex.

"I knew nothing," she said in perfect English. "I didn't even know what menstruation was. I remember when I started my first period, I was sure I was dying. The nuns told me, "Stay away from boys," and they sent me home to talk to my mother.

"Mother gave me a box of pads and one of those belt things and told me the nuns were right, I had to stay away from boys from then on."

I shook my head in disbelief.

"I met Jean-Paul one afternoon when I went to the movies with a group of girls. He smiled at me and I panicked. I knew I had to stay away from him.

"When we married, he was shocked at how little I knew! He told me not to worry, he would be gentle. I cried, of course, mostly out of shame at my own stupidity."

I made sympathetic sounds, and we laughed together. It felt very grown-up being there with Carole, who wasn't much older than I was, discussing adult things like sex and marriage.

I didn't confide my own experiences, though. They would have upset her. She was a sweet lady, little more than a girl, who kept a clean home and liked to talk about makeup.

Jean-Paul arrived with a loud "Hello", apologizing for his lateness. "I see you're already here," he said to me. His English was not as good as his wife's. My French was on a par with his English, so I couldn't complain.

"You're looking very pleased with yourself tonight, Ruth," he said. "I hear from your mama you scored well on your exams this term."

"Yes, thank you," I said. "Where did you see Mom?"

"She was at the store," Jean-Paul said. "She and your father are going to the dance tonight at the town hall. I expect we'll see them there after dinner. Will Stephanie be home alone?"

"No. She's baby-sitting for the LeBlanc's tonight."

"I guess everyone will be at the dance," Carole said.

I smiled. Mom had been looking forward to the annual event. She'd bought a new dress – which was unusual, since she was normally frugal – a lovely peacock blue that set off her dark hair and reflected her eyes.

"We'd better get on the road," Carole said. "We'll be late for dinner."

"I'll shave and change my shirt," Jean-Paul said.

"Ruth, there are dinners in the fridge for you and the kids. Just warm them for 45 minutes at 350. And remember, keep the doors locked." A reminder of the recent murder of a five-year-old girl, and the six-year-old who'd just gone missing. As if a community like ours would ever forget something like that....

"Will do."

"Speak English as much you can," she said. "They need to practice. Adrienne is improving with your help."

I smiled. I enjoyed teaching the little ones to speak English. They learned so quickly at that age.

Jean-Paul emerged from the hall, clean and dashing and ready to dance.

"Have fun, you guys," I said, locking the door behind them.

"Come on, *mes enfants*," I said to the kids. "Let's put dinner in the oven and watch cartoons on the English channel."

***

It was 11:30 when I heard their car doors shut in the driveway. I turned down the stereo, expecting them to be right in, but it was a couple of minutes before the key turned in the front door.

"*Bon soir*," Jean-Paul said. "Is everything all right here?"

"Yes," I said. "The kids were great, as usual. They went right to bed after *Murder, She Wrote*. How was the dance?"

"It was wonderful," Carole said, but her eyes didn't look happy. "I could have danced all night...."

"Yes, well, my dear, you will have to dance alone. I'm *fatigué*. It's bed-time for me."

"Stay awhile, Ruth," Carole said, turning up the volume on the stereo. The Supremes belted out their best material. "You don't have to hurry. Dance with me before you leave."

That was an odd request. Surely my parents would be home already, if the dance was over. They would wonder why I was late. They might worry, knowing a child-murderer was on the loose, although I realized I was no longer a child, and hadn't been for some time.

Carole took my hand and led me to the centre of the floor.

"You girls have fun," Jean-Paul said, but he didn't smile. He shook his head and disappeared down the hall.

We danced for three numbers, then Carole stood to change the record. She tilted her head to one side, straining to listen to the silence between songs.

Hearing nothing, she turned the stereo off.

"I guess you'd better go home," she said. "I'm planning to stay up late tonight. If you and Stephanie feel like joining me for a movie, feel free to knock on the door."

The strangeness of her comment was not lost on me. I liked Carole, but she was certainly in an odd mood. I wondered if she'd had too much to drink.

I sighed, reaching for my coat in the hall closet. Going home was not something I looked forward to. I never knew what I would find there, especially if Dad was in his cups.

I pulled my coat around my shoulders. It wasn't a long walk, but it was cold outside. Our house lights were on. We usually used the rear door, so I hurried up the driveway to the back yard.

"Ruth!" a voice hissed at me from behind the garage.

I jumped.

"Stephanie, for God's sake, what are you doing out here?"

"I got home half an hour ago," she said. "They were fighting again. I'm afraid to go in."

"Damn! What did he do this time?"

"It was awful. You must have heard the yelling. It stopped about five minutes ago. I've been waiting for you."

"I didn't hear anything. I was playing music."

Carole and Jean-Paul were the only neighbors within hearing distance. They must have known about the fight. That's why Carole kept me back, dancing to the Supremes. So I wouldn't walk into a war zone.

"I'm going in," I said.

"But Ruth…."

"I've got to. I have to make sure she's all right. Besides," I added, "it's quiet now."

"I'm coming with you."

"You should stay here till I call you."

"No."

I opened the door and listened. Nothing. Then our mother called out, "Is that you, Ruth? Stephanie? Come into the kitchen."

We hesitated, but only for a minute. She was sitting at the table, a late-night cup of tea in front of her. He was nowhere to be seen.

She had a mark on her face, but it wasn't the worst bruise I'd seen on her. She'd been crying. Her eyes were red, but she was calm.

"Go to bed, both of you," she said. "We're leaving in the morning. Don't tell him. He thinks we've made up. Pack only what you need. One bag each. The minute he leaves the house, we go."

"What if he doesn't leave the house?" I asked.

"He's curling with the Cloutiers at 10. He'll leave by 9:30."

We heard his footsteps in the hall and Mom put her finger over her lips.

"I'm going to bed," I said in what I hoped was my normal voice.

"Me, too," Stephanie said. "'Night, Mom."

"Good night, dears."

"'Night, Dad." I raised my voice as he entered the room.

His eyes were dark. Usually by this point he'd be in 'contrite' mode, pleading for forgiveness. Hooded eyes were a bad omen.

He brightened when he saw me, though, my face carefully arranged in a cheerful mask.

"Good night, girls," he said.

We hurried down the hall to our separate rooms.

***

Sleep came sporadically, despite my exhaustion. I was worried, of course, about this latest drama to upset our lives. We'd left him once before, when I was only six. Stephanie never knew the reason. She missed Dad and cried constantly.

I didn't miss him – didn't shed a single tear over our broken family. A few months later when Mom announced we were going back, that's when I cried.

The fight earlier that night had been one of an endless string of episodes. Intervals of peace never lasted for more than a few months. It was true, I was worried, but most of all I was embarrassed. I considered Carole to be a friend. She genuinely liked me – confided to me as if I was an adult. Now, after witnessing my parents in action, I wondered whether she'd ever ask me to baby-sit again.

I played the scene over in my mind. How could I have been so unaware? I'd thought Carole was behaving strangely, insisting we dance together in the living room. Still, it was the most fun I'd had in a while. I'd been happy to linger with her, share in the after-glow of her evening's dancing.

And all the while she'd been *protecting* me – keeping me from returning to the chaos of my home.

How would I be able to face Carole or her husband?

If we left town in the morning, I wouldn't have to face them. We'd be gone. *Au revoir,* baby.

It was time for an escape.

Frustrated by lack of sleep, I checked the time. 2 am. Might as well start packing.

I got up and crossed the floor, pausing at my window. My room faced the back yard, over-looking the forest's edge. I lifted my curtain…

…*and froze!*

Despite the inadequate relief of the streetlights against the night sky, I knew it was him. I recognized his form as he closed the garage door. It made a whining noise, but was not loud enough to wake a sleeping family.

He hadn't turned the light on, but I was able to make out a shovel leaning against the white building. He bent over and picked up a bundle from the ground and hoisted it over his shoulder, then reached for the shovel.

As his free hand grasped the tool, the loose bundle came apart, revealing a tiny ankle and foot. My eyes, accustomed to the faint glow of the streetlights, had no trouble seeing the white running shoe dangling against his dark shirt.

He looked in my direction once. It seemed as if our eyes met, and for an instant fear stopped my heart, but then he turned away. Moving slowly, so as not to make a sound, he stepped toward the forest. I watched until the darkness wrapped its arms around him and his *petite* burden.

***

Mom was true to her word. We left in the morning. Stephanie didn't cry this time. She'd collected her own memories of 'family bliss', enough of them to harden her resolve. We took a cab to the city and from there got on a train. Mom bought lunch and snacks and crossword puzzles to keep us busy.

He knew where to find us, of course. We received a flood of phone calls and letters pleading for forgiveness, begging us to come home, but we never went back. Mom sent only one answer – a letter telling him to leave us alone. Finally, he did.

I never told anyone what I'd seen that night. Mom never mentioned it, and I took my lead from her. I suspect she knew. She'd probably noticed the unexplained bundle in the garage when they got home that night. She might have questioned Dad, asked what it was – I'm betting that's what the fight was about.

It never occurred to me to turn him in, or that other children might die as a result of my silence. I blame my own naiveté at the age of seventeen, my childish belief in unrelated, isolated incidents. And now, of course, it no longer matters.

Eventually, he put his own unique end to the tragedy. He sat down one afternoon at Her feet with a flask of Holy wine for company, watching the cars fly up and down the highway. None of the drivers spotted our turn-off. Mary kept her vigil, making sure they all passed by.

At dusk, our father put his flask into his pocket and blew his brains out with a hunting rifle.

I hope he had the sense to ask forgiveness first.

DOCTOR SHEDIAC

Editor's Note: When a thirty-year-old murder drags Detective Mallory Tosh back into a past she'd prefer to leave buried, she is forced to choose between childhood loyalties and adult conscience, in the case of Doctor Shediac.

Some mysteries are better left unsolved.

Detectives aren't supposed to think that way. We're taught to uncover secrets, to desire the truth, for its own sake.

It's not our job to adjudicate, to navigate the intricacies of crime and punishment, rather to ask questions and follow evidence. And we are expected to do so without reason, purely for the satisfaction of reaching a solution.

But we are human, after all.

Almost every cop has, at one time or another, imagined a case through to its *preferred* conclusion. Allowed himself to fantasize that he is judge and jury–that he knows best what the outcome should be.

But I digress. I'm not here to explore the endless spectrum of evil deeds encountered by the average cop.

I'm here to tell you about only one felony, and one outcome.

I'll happily leave the greater world of crime for others to ponder, and focus instead on the death of a doctor.

He died long ago. It's hard to say, after so many years, whether justice serves any tangible purpose.

But that's not my concern. I'm a cop, not a philosopher.

***

White sand scorched my fingertips.

It was impossible not to gaze at the shimmering length of beach. I found my sunglasses in the pocket of my tailored cotton shirt and settled them onto my nose.

Parlee Beach. Keeper of my earliest memories, both the good and the...well...less fortunate ones.

I'd forgotten some of the details, like how damned hot the sand was, and how the roaring waves threatened to muffle all other sounds, except for the piercing squawks of overhead gulls.

In one regard, at least, my memory had served me: the lacy trim of blistering sand really *did* stretch for miles.

"Where was he found?" I stood and brushed my hands, opening my nostrils to the salty breeze.

The young Mountie from Southeast Division, Shediac Detachment, straightened herself. Rhéanne Blanchette was on the short side for a cop, but had that strength of bearing they train into all new recruits, especially the females.

"There's a grassy knoll farther up, well past the high water mark."

Grassy knoll. I liked the phrase. I looked in the direction of her pointing finger, and could just make out a tail of yellow crime tape fluttering above a ridge.

She puffed her chest and started toward the scene.

I hesitated, reluctant to leave the water's edge. If I hadn't been wearing my good Italian leathers and black wool pants, the crease freshened that very morning by the hotel's dry-cleaning service, I'd have been tempted to walk in the opposite direction. The frothy lure of the whitecaps was powerful.

Instead, I turned and followed the officer.

We crested the ridge, stepping over a short clump of bush. The scene was laid out before us. A handful of RCMP officers from the Cold Case Division in Fredericton milled around a trussed up hole in the sand, about seven feet by five. As we approached, I could see it was deep, dropping approximately ten feet.

"He must have been near the surface, right?" I said, to no one in particular.

A detective in scruffy-looking plain clothes extended his hand. We shook as he answered.

"He might've been planted as much as four or five feet down," he said. "It would've been hard to go much deeper using a shovel, without hitting packed dirt and rock."

"Tosh," I said. "Mallory Tosh, Toronto P.D."

"François Jobin. Fredericton MCU."

"I have to say up front, I'm not here as part of the investigating team."

"No worries. Blanchette filled me in." He nodded at the officer who'd accompanied me to the scene. "She's with the Shediac Detachment, Southeast Division."

I nodded. It had been Rhéanne Blanchette who'd first contacted me through Toronto's 52nd Division. When they found a small, thick leather-bound journal nestled amongst the bony remains, with my mother's name and childhood address printed on the final page, Blanchette had done the legwork, tracking my late mother, and myself, to the Little Apple.

Toronto.

A driver's license recovered from the burial site revealed the victim to be Dr. Jean-Paul Leroux, a Shediac local, who was reported missing in 1981.

My mother's name might not have raised any questions–might have been mistaken for patient information–except for one thing: it was printed in black, firmly pressed ink, a tidy script that indicated frustration to the handwriting experts. Furthermore, her name had been underlined three times with an angry red pen, circled twice by the same pen, and appeared in the calendar notebook on the day before his reported disappearance.

To add a layer of damnation, a note had been scrawled by the same hand, also in red, under her address: *Make her see reason!*

It might not mean anything, but to the eyes of a detective, it screamed of conflict.

And, since Leroux's skull had been brutally smashed in, "conflict" seemed to be the word of the day.

Blanchette hadn't given me much information over the phone. She had a long conversation with my boss, who advised me to fly to New Brunswick and offer my help as a civilian.

My mother, Naomee Tosh, had kept close ties with her Maritime family right up till her death in 2010.

When we were little, Mom took me and my identical twin, Moraine, and much later our youngest sister Grace, "down home" every summer to be with her family. Our mother was a volatile woman, most often reticent and sometimes angry, who likely suffered from a bi-polar disorder. The only time we ever saw her happy was during those summer visits.

My father, Derek Moody, was a Toronto boy. They met in 1981, when Mom came to the city. They never married, but lived together in Wilson Heights area until he died in 2001.

My father was difficult to live with. I can't say he was missed—let's leave it at that.

In my memory, Moraine and I raised each other. She was lovely, feminine, stylish and demure, while I was the tomboy of the family. When Grace came along, we quickly took over her basic care, leaving our mother to tend to her demons.

"Blanchette tells me you've offered to drive up to the Tosh farm with us," Jobin said.

"When do you want to go?"

"This afternoon would be good. Before word gets out. You know how quickly bad news spreads."

He gave me a sideways look, and I hurried to say, "Blanchette asked me to keep it to myself. I haven't contacted any of my relatives."

"Good. Since you're here as a civilian, I'll ask the questions."

"Of course. I'll make the introductions and let you take it from there."

Jobin wasn't being a bully. He was following protocol. I had to be careful not to be perceived as inserting myself into the investigation. After all, my mother, Naomee Tosh, was the only POI we had at the moment.

My capacity had to be strictly off-the-books.

Having a cop on hand who knew the Tosh family well enough to encourage open dialogue, but not well enough to suffer from misguided loyalties, could prove useful for Jobin.

I followed him to the parking lot. I'd rented a Focus—not much muscle, but great on gas. It had been more than fifteen years since my last visit, and I wasn't sure I'd be able to find the farm on my own.

"I'll drive," he said. "We'll come back for your car afterward."

"Good." It made sense, but I missed my Wrangler.

"When was the last time you were at the farm?"

"Jeez, it would've been sometime in the late '90s. My grandmother Bessie Tosh was still alive at the time."

"Was your mother close to the family?"

"Yeah, very close. She brought us home every summer. Her oldest brother, George, took over running the farm. He still lives in the old house, along with his sister, my Aunt

Zelda. Uncle John and his wife Tillie have a new house on the property. They have two grown kids, about my age. Stacia and Robbie. I'm not sure where my cousins live."

"Any other cousins? Aunts or Uncles?"

"Not that I know of, at least not in the Shediac area. Mom did have a younger brother, Harold, but he died in the early '80s. She didn't talk about him much."

I stared out the window, watching the cottages of Vista Street give way to Gould Beach Road, and on to Main Street, past the fried clam stands and the Shediac Lobster Shop. At Chapman Corner we made a right, heading north. When we reached Bae Vista, Jobin hung a left onto 134. It rolled past forests and Acadian farms of varying affluence.

"Almost there," he said. "Did your mother ever talk about Dr. Leroux?"

"I don't think so." I gave the answer almost in my sleep. It hadn't been a long flight, but there is always a huge rigmarole at Pearson International. Then, renting a car in Moncton, hooking up with Blanchette in Shediac....

Not to mention being whacked in the face with the reality of Parlee Beach. The flood of memories. Frankly, it had left me exhausted.

"Shit!" I said, snapping awake.

"What?"

"I just remembered something. It may not be relevant."

"Spit it out, while it's fresh in your mind."

"It's just something I overheard a long time ago. My Uncle John was in his cups. I think he was talking to my mother and Uncle George."

"What did he say?"

"Doctor Shediac. That's all. It was nothing. Just a phrase I remember."

***

Suddenly I was there, on the beach, skipping over the blistering sand with my sister, Moraine.

A pot of lobster was screaming over a fire, and the tables were set with butter, sugared lettuce, potato salad, Maritime baked yellow-eyed beans and coleslaw.

Doctor Fucking Shediac, my Uncle John said.

Settle down, John. My mother had a worried look.

Take it easy. Uncle George caught me in one arm and Moraine in the other, swinging us into a big bear hug. *You girls go for one last swim. We'll be eating soon.*

He dropped us onto the hot sand and we squealed, drowning out the sound of the boiling lobsters.

I hopped from one foot to the other, and was about to race Moraine to the water, when Uncle John staggered around the table, raised his beer in the general direction of a sandy ridge, and said, *Here's to Doctor Shediac, that miserable bastard. May he rest in peace.*

Johnny, knock it off, my mother said. *You've had enough to drink. Tillie, did you bring coffee? Better heat it up.* Mom grabbed the bottle from her brother's hand and emptied it onto the sand.

Moraine and I ran laughing into the ocean.

***

It didn't prove anything.

Regarded in the context of a childish mind, it carried no weight whatsoever.

Just the same, I rolled up my window and crossed my arms over my chest.

"You cold?" Jobin said, closing his window.

"A little." I took a deep breath. "What can you tell me about Leroux?"

"He had a house on the outskirts of Shediac."

"Oh."

"Yeah. In the early '80s he was the only doctor living in the area," he added.

I thought about that.

"He was a heart surgeon. He worked out of Moncton General. He left the hospital late one evening and never made it home."

"Anyone see him leave?"

"Hospital staff remembered saying good night to him. His car never left the lot."

"And that was in 1981?"

"Yes. Late summer."

I did some mental math. My mother, Naomee Tosh, had moved to Toronto in the fall of '81. Moraine and I were born late in '82.

Thanks to my twin's sudden death earlier that summer, my DNA was on file with the Toronto Coroners' office. I quickly ruled out the possibility that Doctor Leroux might have been our father. My DNA had established that my younger sister, Grace, and I had the same father.

Leroux was already dead long before Grace was born.

Disappointed, I had to admit that Derek Moody was my biological father. Much as I might like to deny it, I carried the asshole's DNA.

"We're here." Jobin turned into the winding driveway, parking close to the old house. The new place was visible on the other side of the field, a comfortable distance away.

Aunt Zelda answered the door, looking a little heavier and a lot greyer, but otherwise exactly as I remembered her.

"Mallory, is that you?" she said. She glanced from me to Jobin, and back at me, suspicion clouding her eyes.

"Hi, Aunt Zelda," I said. "It's good to see you."

"What's happened?" she said.

"Don't worry, Aunt Zelda, everything's ok. This is Detective Jobin of the Fredericton RCMP. He just wants to ask a few questions, mostly about Mom. He asked me to come with him."

She recovered, pulling the door open and ushering us into the main parlor.

"When did you get home, dear? Did Gracie come with you? Have you seen your cousins yet? Your Uncles? Oh, it's been so long, you must have so much news."

That was an understatement.

Earlier that summer, my estranged twin, Moraine, who'd been missing for over fifteen years, had died. I learned she'd been living less than three miles from me, under the assumed name of Susan Baxter.

And, wonder of wonders, Moraine/Susan had a daughter! Carolyn Baxter, fifteen years old, was the spitting image of her mother, and by extension, my own mirror image.

My niece, Carolyn, was now living with me.

Yes, I had news.

But now was not the time to get into it.

"Aunt Zelda, Detective Jobin needs to ask some questions. Can I make tea while you and he have a chat?"

"No, thank you, dear. I think you'd better stay with us."

Her face darkened, and it was impossible to guess what she was thinking. She sat in her favorite straight-backed chair, leaving us to sink into the overstuffed armchairs near the fireplace.

"Mrs...." Jobin began.

"Miss. Miss Tosh. I never married, Detective. But you can call me Zelda. That's my name."

A defensive edge had crept into her voice, and my heart sank. Normally, Zelda was the most cheerful, unflappable person I knew.

Because I was raised by an unpredictable mother and a violent father, Zelda was my rock–my proof that there were good, strong minded adults, and that I could, by force of will, become like her.

"Zelda," he continued, "I have to ask you about things that happened a long time ago."

"My memory is exceptional."

"I'm glad to hear it. Back in 1981, when your younger sister, Naomee, was still living here, how old would she have been?"

My Aunt's eyes rolled upward, fixing on the ceiling for a moment. She was doing the math.

"I would have been twenty or twenty-one. Twenty, I think. So Naomee had just turned seventeen."

"Has your family always lived here?"

"We've been right here, on this farm, for generations."

"So you would have known everyone around here."

"Most everyone. If they went to the Anglican Church, or played Bingo, or had kids that went to school with my niece and nephew, or shopped at our supermarket. Of course, a lot of folks around here are Catholic. I'd still know most, at least to see them."

"Do you remember a doctor, a heart surgeon who lived here in the seventies? He had a place near the shore, near Shediac Harbour."

Zelda folded her hands in her lap, giving the question some thought.

"My doctor is in Moncton," she said. "What was this fellow's name? Maybe I'll recognize it."

"Leroux. Jean-Paul Leroux."

She kept her eyes on Jobin's face. "That's a common name around Shediac," she said.

"He would have been in his forties then. A good looking man. Tall." Jobin reached into an envelope and pulled out a photo. It was aged, but still clear. It showed a handsome, stern-looking man with neat dark hair and black eyes. He held it in front of Aunt Zelda.

She took the photo, mulling it over.

"I just don't know," she said. "I might have seen him around, but I don't think I knew him."

"What about your sister?" he said. "Did Naomee see the same doctor as you? Or did she ever mention a friend who was a doctor?"

"If you mean was she dating him, Detective Jobin, my sister was only a girl at the time. This Leroux was a grown man. My family would have put a stop to any funny business. No, I don't remember her ever mentioning a doctor friend."

The back door opened with the same screen-door-squeal that I remembered, and my Uncle George called out, "Zelda, is someone here? I saw a car out front."

"Yes, George, Mallory is here. She's with a detective from Fredericton." Zelda hopped up from her chair and headed for the kitchen, where George was washing up. My Uncle was always careful not to bring dirt from the field into the house with him.

Jobin followed Zelda to the kitchen, making sure she and George wouldn't have a chance to confer privately.

"Mr. Tosh," he said, holding out his hand, while George dried his, "I'm François Jobin. We'll need to speak with you, as well as with your brother, John. Is he here?"

"He's finishing up in the barn, then he'll head over to the new house. I'll try his cell phone. He usually carries it when he's working, in case Tillie needs him."

Uncle George made the call, and within five minutes my Uncle John was washing up in the same kitchen sink. I put on a pot of tea, notwithstanding Zelda's earlier rejection of the idea. I was embarrassed to note that Uncle John had been drinking. He wasn't far gone, but it was early in the day. I knew Aunt Tillie wouldn't approve, though with her good nature, she usually took most things in stride.

"Mallory, my dear," Zelda called in from her chair in the parlor, "would you make a pot of coffee as well? Your Uncle John doesn't care for tea."

"Of course," I said, forgetting my embarrassment as John winked at me. His sense of humor was contagious. I couldn't help but grin.

"Now that you're all here," Jobin said, "we've had an incident over at Parlee Beach. We've found the remains of a fellow who's been dead for some time. I'm wondering whether any of you might know this man." He held the picture out again, and this time Uncle George studied it before passing it to Uncle John.

"Don't know him," George said.

"Good looking fellow," John said, winking at me again. "But can't say I recognize him. Was he from around here?"

"Had a place in Shediac."

I watched their faces, as I'm sure Jobin did. Their placid brows didn't fool me for a moment. I couldn't guess what it was, but they sure as shit were hiding something.

"His name was Dr. Jean-Paul Leroux," Jobin repeated for the benefit of my uncles. "A surgeon out of Moncton General."

What occurred to me at that point was that none of them, not Zelda, George, nor John, had asked the obvious question: What had happened to Dr. Leroux?

Jobin must have caught the omission as well, because he studiously refrained from offering any details.

"There's a Leroux family I know in Riverview," Uncle John said. "They spend a lot of time over in Pointe Du Chêne."

"Haven't been to the Point in years," Jobin said. "I'll track them down. They might be related."

He lifted his teacup, letting a momentary silence build. We cops know how to do that. To let the silence do the asking for us.

With a suspect in hand, you never know how he or she will react to one line of questioning or another.

But they all respond pretty much the same way to silence.

First they twitch.

Then their eyes begin to dart.

This took place in a fraction of a second, my relatives glancing almost imperceptibly at each other, before Aunt Zelda coughed.

"We didn't know this man," she said.

More silence. I was sorely tempted to break it, just to make things easier on my aging relatives, but I knew better than to give in.

"Fellow must have had enemies," John said. He took a long swallow of his coffee. "Fellow gets himself whacked..." He caught himself, but too late to suck back his words.

Jobin looked at me, his eyes flashing.

"Whacked..." he let the word out slowly. "Yes. Fellow gets whacked, he might have enemies."

"We don't know this Dr. Leroux," my Aunt said, standing to let us know the visit was over. "My brothers have been working in the field all day. It's time I got George some dinner, and Johnny, you'd best be getting home to Tillie. You know how annoyed she gets if you're late."

Uncle George stood as well. He was a big man, taller even than Jobin.

"How long will you be in town, Mal?" he asked me. "Are you staying for dinner?"

"Can't tonight, Uncle George, but thank you. I left my rental car over at Parlee, and my niece, Carolyn, Moraine's girl, is waiting for me at the hotel."

"Moraine had a daughter? What are you talking about?" my Aunt Zelda gasped.

"I just found out this summer. We all thought Moraine had died back in the '90s, but it turns out she'd run away. Must have been pregnant when she ran. Carolyn is fifteen, so the timing is right."

"Carolyn," Zelda said.

"I'll be damned!" John said.

"Bring her for dinner," George said.

"I will, I promise," I said. "Tomorrow for sure. We'll be here at four and help Aunt Zelda cook."

"I'll be damned!" John said again.

Jobin waited till we were back on the highway before saying what we both knew.

"They're hiding something. All three of them."

"Yup." I didn't know what else to say.

"I'll have to bring them in," he said.

"I know."

"And you have no idea? You don't know anything about this?"

"Nothing. I swear."

"I believe you," he said, but his eyes had a skeptical look.

Doctor Fucking Shediac. Here's to that miserable bastard. May he rest in peace.

"You'll be seeing them tomorrow?"

"Yes," I said. "I have to introduce them to my niece."

"Give it a shot," he said. "You never know. Maybe they're tired of keeping secrets."

That was something else we learned in Major Crimes. People tire of their secrets. They get weighed down, and eventually they just have to let go.

"I'll do my best."

***

The next day, full of Aunt Zelda's pork chops and rhubarb pie, we all sat in the parlor: Carolyn, Tillie, George, John, Zelda and me.

"So," I said.

Carolyn kept quiet. I'd filled her in on as much as I could guess.

John was sober. That in itself was indicative of how serious the situation was.

"It was a long time ago," Uncle George said.

"Doctor Fucking Shediac," Uncle John said.

"Now, John," Aunt Tillie said.

We all stared at the fire John had built against the evening chill.

Finally, George said, "Mallory, do you really want to know what happened?"

"Yes."

"It was a summer evening," George said. "Right about this time of year.

"Zelda was away somewhere, at one of those girls' camps she was always trotting off to.

"Your mother, Naomee, was too wild for camp. She'd rather scamper around the countryside with me and John."

"She was a great kid," John added.

"That she was," George agreed, "and so was our little brother, Harold. And Lord be praised, Naomee was so fond of him! The sun sang *Good Morning* and *Good Night* just for him, as far as she was concerned."

"They were closest in age of all of us," Zelda said. "They were inseparable."

I knew what it was like to be that close to a sibling. My heart broke for the thousandth time, in memory of Moraine.

George continued telling the story.

"John's buddy at the time, Guy Leblanc, told us about a delivery that was supposed to be made late that night, to the grocery store where he worked. He'd overheard the owner telling his son about it. *Cash,* he'd said, about forty thousand, lined up for a crooked contractor who wanted everything paid that way, and wouldn't take checks.

"Leblanc wanted to roll the safe, but was afraid they'd know for sure it was him, even though they'd never given him the combination. He was good at things like that–getting past locks and such. Also, the timing was bad. He had to take his father north to Bathurst to visit his dying grandfather. His father was half-blind and couldn't drive.

"Guy didn't know the combination, but he was sure the safe would be easy to lift. If the three of us, John, Harold and myself, big strapping fellows, could get it into the trunk of our car, we could hide it in our barn. When Guy got back to town, he could help us open it. Then we could bury it here at the farm. No one would ever find it.

"So off we go, merry as you please–but of course, Harold tells Naomee all about our plans, and she won't be left behind. *You'll need a lookout,* she says, and she's right. It would take the three of us to break in and cart the thing outta there. We'd need someone to watch for the cops."

"Let me just say, I knew nothing about this until after the fact," Zelda said.

"Thank God you came home when you did, Zelda," John said. "We had no idea what to do."

"Anyway, getting back to that night," George said, "we drove one of our old farm cars, with a fast engine and no plates. No one in town would be likely to recognize it. We got into the supermarket all right, without using Guy's key. That would have been too obvious.

"We found the safe, and even managed to get it outta there and into our trunk. Naomee was driving. John and I got into the car, but Harold thought he'd dropped his cigarette pack inside the store. *I've got lots of cigs,* I said.

"My prints'll be all over the pack, Harold said, then he scarpered back into the store.

"We saw him smiling at the glass doorway, waving the cigarette pack like a damn fool."

"That's when we heard the shout," John said. "It was a cop, doing his foot rounds."

"We froze," George said. "We couldn't drive off without Harold, but he was still standing at the doorway, trapped like a deer in headlights. Naomee honked the horn, and Harold came to his senses and ran for the car.

"I was in the front seat with Naomee, and John was in back. John left the door open for Harold. He damn nearly made it, too, but caught a bullet in the chest just before he reached the car. He didn't go down right away. John pulled him into the car, and we hauled ass outta there, burning rubber all the way.

"I got Naomee calmed down and reminded her to stay on the back roads, and to drive at a normal speed. We took Wynwood till we got to Highlandview, then were forced to scoot over to Shediac Road.

"We knew Harold was in serious trouble. We remembered there was a doctor who lived nearby, just outside of Shediac Proper, not far from Sandy Point.

"Well, we banged on that door for damn nearly five minutes, shouting and hollering, till the old bastard finally woke up and stuck his head out the window. We knew he'd more likely open the door for a girl, so Naomee did the talking, pleading for him to help her baby brother.

"We even hauled Harold out of the car, to show the Doctor we weren't making it up. The blood was all over the place. Any fool could see he was bleeding out.

"But the prick wouldn't come to the door. Sent us packing, back to Hub City, with orders to take Harold to Moncton General.

"We had no choice. We dragged our little brother back to the car. We weren't worried about speeding–if the cops caught us, at least they'd get Harold to the hospital lickety-split. But no one stopped us.

"We didn't say a word for miles. Then, somewhere near Miracle Road, John pipes up from the back seat."

"Harold was dead," John said. "He was down on the back seat with his head on my lap. He died in my arms, like an angel, without a whimper. There was no point trying to get to Moncton General."

"They brought him home," Zelda said. "Mom and Dad didn't know what to do. They called me at camp in the morning, and I came straight away and took charge.

"It has to look like an accident, is what I told them. We dug the bullet out of him and laid him out in the field. Dad couldn't do it to his own son, so it was left to me. I drove the little tractor, the one with the bailing fork, and made sure it speared him just enough that the doc wouldn't look too closely. We left the handbrake off, and made it seem as if the thing had rolled into Harold.

"They didn't question the lack of blood. After all, Harold had lain bleeding on that field for hours before we 'discovered' him and rushed him into Moncton.

"That so-called doctor in Shediac never made an appearance. At least, thank God, he never filed a report, either.

"It was put down to 'death by farming accident'. We watched the papers for any report of a cop firing at the store that night. There was a tiny write-up: Police are asking for any information regarding a break-and-enter and the theft of a safe." Aunt Zelda wiped her eyes. She might be stoic, but she did have feelings.

George picked up the thread where she left off.

"The safe," he said, "was empty. Either the owner had moved the money, or there never was any. Either way, we lost Harold for nothing. A few months later, your mother ran off to Toronto and took up with your father." His voice was thick with distaste for Derek Moody. "Naomee couldn't stay on our old farm without her baby brother."

"Naomee was never the same after Harold died," Zelda said.

"What happened to Doctor Shediac?" I asked.

"We tried to talk to him, but he wasn't at home," John said. "We figured he must work out of Moncton General. His name was Leroux–Doctor Jean-Paul Leroux. Turns out he was a top heart surgeon. Would've been able to save our boy easily, if he'd given a rat's ass."

I bit my lip. It was obvious to me that Leroux had done the only thing he could, under the circumstances. If caught treating a fugitive "off the record", he would almost certainly have risked losing his medical license.

But my uncles would never understand that.

"Did you talk to him?" I pressed.

There was a silence, but I let it build, knowing few people can resist the urge to fill a void.

It was Aunt Zelda who finally spoke.

"Naomee," she said, averting her eyes. In fact, I couldn't help noticing the entire family was avoiding my stare.

"She wouldn't let it go," John said.

"She was closest to Harold of all of us," George said. "She was crazy with grief. She said we had to talk to the doctor, to let him know our brother died because of him.

"We tracked Leroux down at the hospital. We caught him in the parking lot, at the end of his rounds."

"I'd had a few beers," John said.

"We both had," George said. "Anyway, we tried to talk to Leroux. He got pissy and told us to bugger off.

"Next thing we knew, Naomee had a tire iron in her hands. We didn't even know there was one in the car."

"She was out of her mind," John said. "It was over in minutes."

"Then we had to get rid of the body," George said.

"I told them to take it up to Parlee Beach at night," Aunt Zelda said. "There was a place where the kids don't play much, shrouded behind a ridge and some bushes. I told them to go as deep as they could."

My niece, Carolyn must have been shocked by the tale. To her credit, she didn't show it. She sipped her tea, tucking her feet under her.

I looked at my aging relatives, saw the pain, the obvious remorse…the grief that never goes away.

I could understand the rage they'd felt against the person they held responsible for their brother's death.

One day I hoped to find out what really happened to my twin, Moraine, and when I learned the truth, well…let's not draw that scene out to its conclusion.

I could understand what my mother had done. I could sympathize with her desire to avenge Harold. To cut herself a big slice of revenge, even though, deep down, she must have known it wasn't really the doctor's fault, what had happened to her brother.

I could understand it. But I couldn't cover it up.

Secrets, in my experience, are the very imps of evil.

It was time to nail this one to the gates of hell.

INVASION

from the point of view of a journal

It's an invasion of privacy, that's what it is. He holds me in grubby hands, turning me about. He splays me like a fish, only to slam me shut when he doesn't like what he finds.

Words, beautiful words... the bond we shared, she and I. She used to tell me all of her thoughts and dreams. But that was in another lifetime, before the jealousy and rage. Before HE came.

Now it's barely a flake of her life I'm privy to. But what I see is more than enough...

His mood changes, although he doesn't say a word. It's in the way his hands press against me. This must be what she felt when he tried to kill her, hands wrapped around her neck, fingers pressing, stars exploding behind her eyes, welcoming her to the land of perpetual night.

He curses. What is it? His filthy thumb has left a mark on me. Knowing she will understand his villainy, he scrubs it, but I hold firm. I will not let it be erased.

At last — proof!

A door opens in another room. It must be her.

He shuts me quietly, setting me on the nightstand. So clever. She will never suspect he's been violating me, using me as catalyst for his violence.

She moves slowly, in no hurry to greet him. Words are spoken. He leaves me and I hear the refrigerator door.

She joins me, sits on her bed, too weary for tears. There were tears last week, though, the day she told me she was pregnant. It should have been a happy occasion. Instead she wept, smearing ink with salty drops, finally shredding the page.

She reaches for me. *Ah, dear friend, so well I feel your pain.* Even in her grief, her touch is loving. She turns to that last page – sees his mark...

For a moment her eyes are wide at the extent of his invasion, then resignation reclaims its rightful place. Reaching for her pen, she writes a final whisper, laying the words out over his mark:

There must be something more to life than this.

THE NIGHT SHE DIED

A Halloween story

"Hand me that basket, will you, please?"

I reached past Annie to the large wicker basket filled with bite sized chocolate bars: Caramilk, Mars and Snickers.

Grace took it from me without looking up. She was generous with the little ones, placing two bars and some chips in each bag.

It was October 31, 1974. A warm day had produced a clear evening, perfect for costumes and candy.

The skeleton said 'thank you' in a high-pitched voice. The princess just turned and ran, nearly tripping over her frothy skirt.

"Look at those guys," Annie said, pointing at the house next door where a cluster of six children were lined up. They were dressed in home-made costumes – four witches and two warlocks.

Grace laughed, her jowls swaying like heavy fruit in the wind. Not long ago, our cousin had been a beautiful woman. People had compared her petite frame, long dark hair and contagious smile to Audrey Hepburn. In the early '70s, Audrey's trademark sprightly outfits and mannerisms were no longer stylish. Just the same, as a teen, Grace had played up the similarities by dressing in pedal pushers and fun tops.

In '71 Grace married her high-school sweetheart. With the first of three children on the way, it seemed like the thing to do. Frank got a job at one of the big grocery stores, so they weren't suffering for money. They bought a two-story house on a tree-lined street in our little Maritime city and settled in to make a life.

Three years later, with the second baby not yet walking, people no longer mistook Grace for Audrey. An addiction to cola, chocolate and the Colonel's secret recipe had taken care of that.

We still loved her, though. So when our mother asked Annie and me to help Grace out with the little ones for a few days, we jumped at the chance to sleep on her fold-out couch. Frank was out of town at a grocers' convention and Grace, though we didn't realize it at the time, was pregnant with baby number three.

The coven of witches flew up the stairs to Grace's porch and we resumed our shelling out duties. Baby Sara watched the children with wide eyes, wiggling in her infant-seat on the porch. Grace's toddler Lily helped with the candy, solemnly making sure each child got the same amount.

"These are great costumes," Grace said, touching a pointy, silk-covered hat on one of the girls. "Did your Mom make these?"

"Yes," the little witch said. She smiled and we all laughed.

"I can't tell who you are," Grace said. "Your faces are painted so well, I think you really must be witches. Is that Shelly Small I see under that hat? And Tracey?"

The girls giggled.

"What about me, Mrs. Lefebvre? Can you tell who I am?"

"No, indeed, I don't think I can! Oh, wait a moment... Is it Candice Howard? And is this your little sister Haley? Oh, my goodness, how you girls have grown! I hope you won't cast a spell on me."

Grace doled out a generous helping of empty calories to each of the four girls. The two boys held back shyly.

"Come on, Ricky," Grace said. "We like wizards, too! Brent, I know that's you. What a clever wizard you are!" The boys smiled, holding their bags up. It was obvious the children adored our kind-hearted cousin.

"Thank you, Mrs. Lefebvre!" they shouted.

"You're welcome, dears. Say hi to your Mommies for me!"

Everyone loved Grace. She stood only five feet tall and weighed close to three hundred pounds, but it was three hundred pounds of class and heart. In his private moments, Frank must have resented this sudden physical change in his young wife, but he never complained. Adversity is commonplace in the Maritimes. You learn to live with it.

I've often wondered what caused our cousin to balloon up so suddenly. Why the gallons of cola, the compulsive eating? Her parents were wonderful people. I don't believe her problems were rooted in her childhood.

The coven scattered, leaving Grace, Annie and me to chat on the porch while we waited for the next batch of goblins. It wasn't late, but darkness takes hold early in the fall. The streetlights shed small grey rings onto the pavement, struggling in vain to illuminate the area. Of course, we had the porch light on and the walk-up was lined with jack-o-lanterns we'd helped Grace carve earlier.

Still, we were surprised when a young woman, maybe seventeen, stepped out of the night and climbed the stairs to stand in front of us. Her face was pale and her long, sandy-blonde hair fell in front of her eyes. That's the way we all wore our hair back then. After all, the year was 1974. Coifed curls were passé.

The girl had narrow hips and a fragile waist. I wondered where she stored her food; she appeared to have no stomach or bowels.

The smile disappeared from Grace's face, sinking into in the perpetual frown of her under-chin.

"It's you," she said, "again."

The girl didn't answer. She wasn't carrying a trick-or-treat bag, nor was she wearing a costume. She had on a tight-fitting zip-up sweater with the hood down, her long straight hair catching the light. She stared at me through translucent silver eyes.

Eyes are a feature I tend to notice. In fact, with my own non-descript hazel pair, I often find myself envious of women who have remarkable eyes.

Annie's eyes, for example, were perfect for her face – an uncompromising Chelsea blue that never wavered.

Grace had always been known for her perfectly sculpted, huge dark eyes. They were downright exotic, like those of an Arabian princess. Even in her obese state, Grace's eyes were still noteworthy. Movie-star eyes, that's what they were.

This strange girl on the porch, though, blew them both out of the water. In my entire life, both before and since that night, I've seldom seen anything quite like her eyes.

She looked through each of us in turn. Judging us.

Standing wasn't easy for Grace, especially lifting herself up from the low steps where we had been sitting, but she managed. She looked down on the strange girl, her heavy arms shaking with…what was it? Anger? Fear?

Annie stood beside Grace and I followed suit. Whatever was happening, we were united with our cousin.

"You get on home," Grace said to the girl. "Don't you come out here tonight. Go home to your mother, right now!"

The girl looked directly at Grace. The other-worldly look left her silver eyes, transforming her. I watched as the subtle change took effect, altering her into a mere girl – haunted and sad, yes, but otherwise quite ordinary.

"You heard me, now," Grace said, shaking her finger. "Don't you dare come back."

The girl turned away, but before she did I saw a tear shining under the porch light. She straightened her back and walked down the stairs. In the next instant, she was gone – the darkness had absorbed her once again.

***

We helped Grace gather up the candy and blow out the candles in the pumpkins.

"I'm glad you girls are here," she said. "I just can't stand to be alone on Halloween. With Frank gone…"

Annie looked at me, but I was too young to catch the undercurrent of Grace's words. I didn't know that Grace and Frank were on the rocks.

Now, of course, many years later, I understand why Grace had pleaded with our mother to let her bring the kids to our house, why she couldn't bear to be alone on Halloween.

My mother had problems of her own contending with my father's drinking. His volatility was a closely guarded family secret. Mom couldn't let Grace and her children stay with us, so she offered to send us to Grace's house instead.

In October of 1974 I was thirteen years old. Like many teens, I was not particularly good at tuning in to the drama that surrounded me.

Annie, on the other hand, was an empathetic soul. She often understood things I didn't grasp.

"Who was that girl?" I asked.

"It doesn't matter," Grace said, still shaking. She sat on the couch, struggling to breathe slowly, beads of perspiration on her forehead.

"Can we get you anything?" Annie said.

"Yes. There's a glass of Coke in the fridge. Would you get that for me please?"

Annie ran to get the sugary drink that would one day send our cousin to an early grave. We had no way of knowing Grace's sugar consumption would kill her.

"That girl..." Grace began, speaking slowly, "...the first time she came here was three years ago, right after Frank and I got married. I was pregnant with Lily. Frank was off at one of his conventions. She came up the stairs as I was handing out candy, just like she did tonight. You both saw her, right?"

She looked at us, suddenly doubting whether we'd actually seen the girl.

We nodded.

"She was nervous that night," Grace continued. "She was with a group of children, maybe three or four. I thought she was an older sister or something. But when they ran off, she walked down the steps without a word and headed in the opposite direction. I didn't think much of it at the time."

She took a long drink of her cola. My stomach turned, watching her consume the flat, sweet beverage, but she didn't seem to mind it.

"Later that night," she continued, "the girl came back. It was around midnight. I was alone and pregnant. I didn't know what to do."

"What happened?" Annie said, sitting next to Grace and rubbing her back.

"We never lock our doors around here. At least we never used to. The girl pounded on the front door. I ran out to see what was going on, but before I could answer the door she was already standing in the hallway.

"I asked her what she wanted. She frightened me. You girls remember how tiny I used to be?"

We nodded again, waiting for Grace to continue.

"She said she just wanted to stay awhile. To talk with me. I could tell she was nervous. But I didn't think about that. All I could think was that I wanted her to leave. You've seen her eyes. She looks like a witch. She scared the be-Jesus out of me."

"Anyone would be scared," I said.

"Did she leave?" Annie asked.

"Not right away. She came into the living room and sat on the couch. She kept saying 'Just let me stay a couple of minutes. I won't bother you.'

"I got the broom out of the hall closet and shook it at her. 'You have to go,' I said. Finally she got up and made for the door. The second she was outside, I locked it behind her, then I ran to the back door and locked it, too. I made sure the windows were locked. Then I sat on this couch in the dark, praying she wouldn't come back.

"She must have stayed on my porch, that's all I can think. I honestly believed she'd left."

Our cousin was still shaking. She took another long drink of cola and shut her eyes.

"Did she come back?" Annie asked.

I drew in a sharp breath, waiting for the answer.

"Yes. Either she came back, or she had never left. I'm not sure which. I finally fell asleep on the couch around 12:30. I woke up again around 1:00."

"What happened?"

"I-I just can't talk about it anymore," Grace said. "I've pleaded with Frank to sell the house – to move out of this neighborhood. But we both grew up here. He says we can't afford to move.

"Come on, now," she added, shaking her head. "Let's send the little ones to bed before they get all wound up."

I glanced at Lily, the oldest, who had come into the room and was sitting on the other side of Grace, clutching her mother's arm.

By 11:00 both children had long since fallen asleep and we got Grace settled into her bed with a sleeping pill.

"It's the only way I'll get any rest," she explained. "Annie, would you check the door one more time?"

"I will."

"And don't forget the back door. Please."

"I will."

Annie had more patience than I could ever lay claim to. Grace had already insisted that she check all of the doors and windows. Obediently, she'd gone from one to the other without a word.

We watched Grace slip into a drugged slumber before we finally went back to the living room to make up our couch-bed.

"Holy crap!" Annie whispered.

"I know," I said.

Annie's blue eyes sparkled in the darkness as she pulled the covers up, trying to make a cocoon. Sleeping with my sister was enough to make me homicidal. She was a terrible blanket hog – with no remorse whatsoever.

I sighed and stomped off to find another blanket.

"Grace is terrified," Annie said.

"Me, too!"

"I think she's lost her mind. Seeing that girl is playing tricks on her."

"Yeah. I wonder if she's imagining the whole thing."

We tried to sleep. Annie drifted off for a moment, but every passing car, every creak in the old house, had us both wide-eyed once again. Finally we gave up and just lay there, whispering girl secrets to each other to take our minds off the shared sense of impending terror.

We'd only been asleep a short time when we woke to the sound of pounding on the door. I jumped out of bed, but Annie said "No, leave it. Just ignore it."

Before I could climb back into bed, the girl was in the hallway.

"I thought you locked the door," I said.

"I did." Annie was the brave one. She was used to sound and fury, having taken more than her share of our father's crap. She jumped out of bed and positioned herself between me and the nervous intruder.

"What do you want?" Annie said. I could feel her body tensing up the way it always did when she stared down the old man. Bracing for the blow.

"I just want to talk to you. Can I come in?"

"No. This isn't our house. We have babies sleeping here. You have to go." Annie took a step toward the girl.

Our visitor had other ideas. She pushed past my sister and sat on the edge of our bed.

"Just let me stay a few minutes," she said. "I won't bother anyone. You both go back to sleep and I'll just sit here quietly."

My gut churned the way it always did when I was afraid. I worried I'd lose control of my bowels. Annie once again placed herself between me and the girl.

"You have to go," she said. She was calmer now, her voice quieter, more gentle. "I'm sorry, but this isn't our house. You can't stay."

The strange girl got up slowly and crept back to the door, staring at Annie, hoping for a change of heart.

"Go home, now," Annie said.

With that the girl was gone.

An hour later we were still restless, drifting in and out of sleep, each wrestling for control of the blankets. We weren't talking anymore – we were way too tired for that. We were in 'hunker down' mode, praying for the long night to pass.

Even though we were half-expecting something more to happen, the man's voice still startled us when it shattered the eerie stillness.

"There you are!" he shouted. He was in the laneway beside our cousin's house, just outside the living room.

There was pounding on the door and the girl's voice, frantic now, pleaded with us to let her in. Before we could respond, the knocking stopped. We heard footsteps taking the porch stairs two at a time.

"Where were you tonight?" the strange man shouted. "I asked you a question. Who were you with? What were you doing?"

"Please… leave me alone," the girl said.

There was a scuffle. Annie banged on the front window and shouted, "Leave her alone! I'm calling the police!"

Annie reached for the phone. There was a loud thump as the girl jumped off the porch and another as the man followed her, filling the night air with his angry curses.

He caught the young girl easily. She squealed as he pounded her against the wall of the house. Our cousin's side window was small and high, so I couldn't see into the laneway, but the noises were deafening as he beat the defenseless teen with inhuman force.

I couldn't move. I looked at Annie where she stood holding the phone, a mixture of horror and fury on her face.

The shouts and the beating continued for maybe five minutes.

Then silence.

No more squeals. No more curses. Even the girl's whimpering had stopped. In the stillness the house continued to shake, or maybe it was just the blood pounding in my ears.

"Stand up," the man's voice said. "Come on. Quit playing with me. Get on your feet."

No response from the girl.

Then I heard his footsteps as he ran away, up the alley and gone, just like that.

Five minutes later the police arrived. They pounded on the front door.

This time Annie opened it.

It took twenty minutes for them to question us. During that time, an officer tried to wake my cousin, but couldn't get a rise out of her. They searched the neighborhood to put our minds at ease, but you could tell they were just going through the motions. They'd been called to my cousin's house before. There was no battered girl in the alleyway, no violent man to place under arrest. In fact, all that remained was the shared sense of a lingering nightmare.

Maybe we really had dreamt the whole thing...

The police did their duty: took our statements and went on their way.

***

Thirty-six years have passed since that night at my cousin's house. My sister died a few years after that. Teen suicide. Not surprising, given our family life.

Frank ran off in 1980 and took the three kids with him, shacking up with a clerk from his grocery store. I never blamed him, even though I knew it tore Grace apart. His new wife, Shirley, was an older woman who chain-smoked, treated his children well and promised to never, never let herself get overweight.

I've been married and divorced twice – both times going in with high hopes. I've now come to grips with the fact I wasn't meant for matrimony. I haven't got the patience.

As for Grace, the diabetes finally got her. She died last week, drowned, more like it, in cola and potato chips. She was nearly four hundred pounds, a shuddering mass of grief and loneliness. And remorse. She'd been in a nursing home since Frank left, no longer able to climb the stairs in their house.

***

Our family moved away from the Maritimes when I was in my teens. With thousands of miles between us, I'd long since lost touch with my ailing cousin. I thought of her often, though. When I got the call from Lily saying her Mom had died, I caught the first plane home.

Frank was at the funeral. He looked like a broken man. He left Shirley's side to greet me, his eyes searching mine for forgiveness. There was nothing to forgive. It wasn't his fault Grace had died. She'd killed herself, like my sister only more slowly. More painfully, but just as surely.

"I only wish Grace could've been happier," he said. "She was always smiling when we were kids. She laughed all the time. Everyone loved our Grace."

"That's true," I said, wondering how the years could have fooled us all so thoroughly.

I glanced around the room and spotted their youngest son, Andy, whom I recognized from pictures, standing next to his sister, Sara. Andy was slightly overweight. Sara, on the other hand, was stunning – the spitting image of Audrey Hepburn, right down to the tiny frame and the curve of her delicate jaw. It was like looking at Grace in the early days.

Sara glanced my way and the exotic beauty of her eyes took my breath away – dark pools in an ivory face.

Grace's youngest children were fast approaching middle age. The realization shook me.

Frank was saying something, so I turned to face him.

"It was that girl," he repeated, gripping my hand. "Do you remember? The teenager that was murdered outside our house in '71."

"I remember," I said. Back then we didn't have the internet, but after the incident we'd experienced in '74, Annie and I had scoured the public libraries looking for reports of her death. Her name had been Alison Carter. An ordinary name. An ordinary girl.

Unless you remembered her eyes – those silver shafts of light that went right through you, that saw your every weakness and condemned you for the coward that you were.

"Grace always blamed herself," Frank said. "Always said if only she'd let the poor girl stay awhile, she wouldn't have been killed."

"Grace was pregnant and afraid. She was not much more than a child herself. A pregnant nineteen-year-old."

"I know," he said. "But she never got over it. Every year on Halloween she dreamt the girl came back. The guilt destroyed her."

"It wasn't her fault," I said. "She didn't murder the girl."

And what about Grace's kids? I wondered. Had they been damaged, too, by the wraith-like vigilante who stalked their mother?

Andy and Sara stood together, holding hands, two beautiful adults who looked just like their parents.

I searched the room, finally spotting the oldest, Lily, alone in the corner. I joined her. She recognized me and held out her hands.

She was taller than Grace had been – around five-seven – and stood erect. Her sandy blond hair fell long and straight, adding to her height.

"Hello, Jane," she said.

"Hi, Lily. How have you been?"

I knew Lily had spent a lot of time with Grace in the final years. She was probably closer to her mother than anyone else had been. Still, there were no tears in her eyes, nor was there a catch in her voice when she spoke.

"I've been ok," she said.

I looked away. Frank was standing at his wife's side near the over-sized casket. I wanted to join them, to leave Grace's oldest daughter alone with her thoughts.

Lily made me mildly uncomfortable. Something about her always had. It was just too hard, seeing those silver eyes that looked right through me. It was too hard knowing…what I knew — what Grace must also have known.

Lily smiled and touched my hand, trying to relieve my anxiety.

"It's ok now," she said. "I've forgiven her."

SPRING'S LAST SKATE

Northern Quebec in March, where birch trees stand snowy white against a sky that is bluer than sapphire, more pure in its color than the blue of Martha's eyes. Clean snow crunched under my boots, its surface just beginning to surrender to the sun's caress.

Off to our left, a ditch transformed itself into a tinkling stream, fed by rivulets from the melting banks. Spring thaw – nature's concession – one more chance at life in a region that spends too much energy on dying.

Martha reached for my hand. My red mitten was torn at the thumb, but I didn't mind. The fabric was soaked anyway from playing in the snow. It smelled of wet wool, the deep, organic musk of animal.

My sister's touch was warm, as always, even through the fabric.

I let her lead me home, despite the brilliant sunshine that called on us to keep playing, despite the cheerful voices of the children at the rink across the street. Days like that don't come along often. Their rarity burrows into the grey matter that secures our memories, staking out permanent pockets filled with mental photographs we can recall at any time, regardless of the slippery passing of the years.

Images to hold forever… a black rock jutting from the snow… a jack pine bent against frozen clouds… a worn mitten, offering a gay dash of red in the sunlight… the stuff of recollection.

"Hurry up, Doris," Martha said, pulling at my arm.

I knew the drill. At eight and six years old respectively, Martha and I enjoyed more freedom than many children. Our village in the far north still believed 'crime' was something

71

you watched on television, so long as the cable didn't go out. We were free to run without supervision, skating, crafting snowmen and building forts in the little woods from bits of rotting lumber dumped by lazy contractors at the edge of the larger forest.

There was one caveat to our boundless freedom: we must not be late for meals. *Le déjeuner*, lunch, would be ready at noon sharp. The undeniable pleasure of dallying in the morning air was not worth our mother's annoyance.

I did my best to keep up, short legs hindered by the snow pants we were forced to wear. They, too, were soaked through, but our mother would toss our over-clothes into the dryer while we ate, so they'd be ready for us to wear by afternoon.

Martha let go of my hand.

"Wait for me," I said.

She relented, taking my hand again and pulling me toward our house.

We paused at the driveway. It had been ploughed earlier in the week, but the previous day's fresh snow in the blue-grey shadow of a spruce still showed our childish footprints from the morning. Our mother would probably ask us to shovel the drive later, before the afternoon became too cold.

I saw but didn't really notice the larger prints, blue-white impressions moving first to the front door, then back again.

Our father had died in the fall. Our mother did not entertain guests, unless you counted a handful of neighbor ladies who came in rotating shifts to drink coffee. They were good women, who knew the erosion loneliness could cause on a spirit. They did their best to make sure our mother did not become a casualty of her own company.

She never complained, but we knew she missed Dad. Her eyes would light up when we told her of a pending school concert or a parent-teacher meeting – anything to

72

break the monotony of endless evenings spent in adult limbo with only two small girls for conversation.

Forgetting it was Saturday, I assumed the boot prints belonged to the mailman, a great burly Quebecois with the nature of a jolly lumberjack who had a smiling wife and three children of his own. His oldest was being scouted by the NHL.

"Look," Martha said. She pointed at the prints. They led to the front door, back to the drive, stopped about half-way down the driveway then turned and went into the back yard.

I nodded, thinking it was strange, but we were only children, after all, innocent to the possibilities a pair of heavy footprints in the snow could imply. Hungry, we opened the unlocked front door and stepped into the hallway, careful to strip our wet outer-wear before following the rich smell of barley into the kitchen.

"Your cheeks are rosy," our mother said, dishing hot soup into bowls. "Eat up quickly. This will warm you. Then you can go outside again."

"My snow pants are wet," I said.

I expected her to hop up and throw them into the dryer, but instead she said, "You can wear your other pair. That way you won't have to wait. Now eat up."

My other pair was too small, but I knew better than to argue. Even after my father's death, in the height of her grief, our mother was nothing if not 'determined'.

She was a loving, gentle woman, who filled her days with cooking, cleaning, sewing and caring for her girls. Just the same, she brooked no nonsense from either of us.

We ate our soup with slices of fresh-baked bread, which Mom buttered quickly, and sipped our hot chocolate.

"Come on," she said. "You're missing the whole day. Both of you – go wash your faces and use the bathroom. Take your skates and head over to the rink."

She smiled, but there was something anxious in her blue eyes. I didn't make much of it. Six-year-olds are not known for their empathy. Besides, since our father's fatal heart-attack in September, anxiety had become a common visitor in our house.

She tucked me into the tight snow pants while Martha dressed herself. Then she shooed us through the front door, not even pausing to glance at the heap of wet things on the floor.

"Stay out for a while," she said. "The weather's way too nice to be indoors. Do some skating before the ice gets choppy."

We waved. I was wearing a dry coat and a pair of bright yellow mittens Mom had made for me earlier that year. My skates were second hand, but they looked new and they fit me well.

Martha had on a blue nylon coat and a pair of new hand-made mittens – lamb's wool as blue as the March sky, as blue and as innocent as her own eyes.

That was the last time we saw our mother alive.

CORNER STORE

I've done many things in my thirty-one years. Some good; some falling short of noble.

If there's one deed, or rather 'un-deed' that still fingers the chords of my memory, one oversight I wish I could put right, it would hearken back to a day sixteen years ago in our local convenience store.

To a girl by the name of Angelina Salvaggi.

It's an excuse to say I was only fifteen at the time. Even then, I was no child, not really. In truth, Penelope Canon has never been naïve.

I was fully aware that child needed my help. I just didn't know how to give it.

Aunt Rachel, send me once again to the corner store for milk. Let me go back in time, as if those sixteen years had never happened. Lend me your personal road map, the one that makes you always do the right thing, even though you're half-crazy at the best of times.

Let me do that day again. Maybe this time I'll be a better person.

***

Something didn't feel right.

The store was empty, except for me. It was dimly lit but clean, smelling of fresh bread, candy and a hint of vinegar.

I walked to the back where they kept the milk in tall coolers. At fifteen I was small, still am, in fact, but in good shape. I lifted the heavy bag with ease.

The owner, Sam Salvaggi, would normally be behind the counter. He lived with his family above the store. A pleasant man – always ready with a smile and a kind word.

There were two doors at the back of the store, near the dairy coolers. The door on the left led upstairs to the family home. The one on the right led into the storage area behind the refrigerators.

As I carried the milk to the front of the store, Sam's eight-year-old daughter, Angelina, appeared. She came through the storage room door on the right of the coolers. I remember wondering what she'd been up to back there.

She was upset. Her eyes were red and she wouldn't look at me, even when I said *hello*.

She walked quickly, eyes down, through the store and out the front door, into the afternoon sunshine.

A few seconds later Sam, a man of mid-to-late thirties, came through the same door. He nodded, not looking at me, and followed me to the checkout counter.

"Good afternoon, Miss Canon," he said, regaining his composure and meeting my gaze. "Lovely day out there."

His smile was friendly if forced, and I put aside my uncomfortable thoughts of his crying daughter.

"It's perfect. Wish it could stay like this all summer."

"How is your Aunt?"

"She's well, thank you."

"Say hello for me. Tell her I'm expecting the new knitting magazine any day now."

My Aunt Rachel loved to knit. Unless you enjoyed being ridiculed at school, you couldn't wear anything she made, but that didn't slow her down. Sam Salvaggi had a standing order for her favorite crafting magazines, and always set aside a copy for her when they arrived.

"I'll let her know."

I paid for the milk. It was a short walk home to Aunt Rachel's house down the street. I took my time, mulling over the encounter. Something nagged at the back of my mind, telling me I should find the girl, ask her if she was all right.

But I didn't do it. Instead I got distracted, as we sometimes do.

"Is that you, Penelope?"

"Yes, Aunt Rachel."

"Good. Dinner's ready. How was school?"

I put the milk away and sat down to one of my Aunt's eclectic meals, this one a strange assortment of undercooked greens and overcooked meat beside a slice of leftover pizza.

Aunt Rachel was no friend of Martha Stewart. On my Aunt's table, presentation took a back seat to convenience every time.

I thought about mentioning the corner store encounter to my Aunt, but I was hungry and the pizza was good, and frankly I forgot.

Shortly after that, Aunt Rachel sold the West End house and we moved to a condo in the East End of Toronto.

I thought about Angelina Salvaggi occasionally. Sometimes I'd dream about her – in a nagging, guilty kind of way. But for the most part I was able to push that memory down into the place where I stored my personal regrets.

Until now, sixteen years later.

It was Saturday morning, and on Saturdays I'd pick up the paper on my way to visit Aunt Rachel at the condo for brunch.

Usually I would cook, badly. We had that in common.

Something about the story made me feel uneasy.

I couldn't put my finger on it at first, but then I recognized the name in the caption: Salvaggi. It was an unusual one.

The photo alone wouldn't have triggered my memory. After all, the sad but beautiful young woman on the front page of *The Saturday Star* bore no resemblance to that little girl from long ago.

Once I made the connection, I imagined I saw something familiar in her eyes, some look she'd retained from childhood.

I held the paper out to my Aunt.

"What is it, Penelope?" she asked, taking *The Star*.

"The girl. Do you remember her?"

"Salvaggi…. The name is familiar."

"They owned the corner store near our old house, on Wayburn."

"Oh, yes, I remember. Lovely family. Always had fresh bread and milk. The wife liked to knit." She read the headline aloud. "Daughter returns home to nightmare."

"You remember that home invasion in the West End last week? They didn't release the family name at the time. According to the story, the daughter was in Acapulco with her boyfriend when it happened."

"What a thing! She must be devastated. What was her name again?"

"Angelina," I said.

"She had an older brother, right?"

"Apparently he was one of the victims. Mother, father and brother. Police haven't released all the details, but it sounds like it was particularly brutal."

"Murder always is," Aunt Rachel said. "And to lose everyone… the poor girl."

"Yes."

***

That night I dreamed I was alone in the store. I rang the bell for service, but no one came. I had a shopping basket full of chocolate bars and Twinkies.

I rang the bell again, frustrated. Looking for the owner, I wandered to the back where they kept the milk. I spied the door on the right, the one that led to the storage area behind the tall coolers.

Suddenly I was tiny, even smaller than I am in real life. I had to reach up for the door handle. I turned it, but no one was in the storage room. The family lived in an apartment above the store, so I went to the door on the left, opened it and called upstairs, hoping to rouse someone.

Still no one came.

In a hurry to leave that disturbing place, I pulled out a twenty and set it on the counter, under the bell. I reached across the counter for a plastic bag, intending to fill it with my purchases.

But when I looked in the basket, there were no chocolate bars, no Twinkies.

Instead, staring up at me, was a head.

My own.

I woke, unable to shake a sense of horror. My inaction years earlier had obviously planted seeds of guilt.

It was too late to help the child Angelina. Whatever she may or may not have suffered back then, those days were gone.

So was her immediate family.

Still, I felt an urge to seek her out. To help the adult, if there was any way I could.

As a private investigator, maybe I could call on my rather tenuous contacts to gather the details the police were holding back.

What good was it having friends on the force if a girl couldn't get the 'inside scoop' once in a while?

It was probably that kind of reasoning that made me so popular with Toronto's finest.

Hell, why stop being objectionable now? I had a reputation to protect.

Detective Darryl Francis answered on the first ring. He sounded tired.

"Got time for lunch today?" I said.

"Maybe. What's it about?"

"I'm hurt, Darryl. Can't I just buy a cop a donut now and then without having my motives scrutinized?"

He didn't laugh. Not everyone gets my sense of humor.

"I'm kind of busy today, Penelope. Is it important?"

"It's about the Salvaggi case."

"Oh."

***

We met at the Courtyard Restaurant in Yorkville. Darryl is fond of Schnitzel and I like the owners, even though it's usually too much to eat and they bring soft drinks in cans.

I usually get three meals for my money.

"What's your interest in the case?" he asked.

"I used to know the family. Not well. I grew up in their neighborhood. They owned the corner store."

"Have you heard from them lately?"

"Not for years. But I'd like to help the daughter, if I can. She was a nice girl."

He chewed on that for a minute.

Finally he said, "So you're not on tab?"

"No. Just a citizen, hoping to help a former neighbor."

"In that case, I think you should stay out of it."

That caught me off guard, and I looked at him, with noodles dripping red sauce down my chin.

"Seriously, Penelope. If you're not already in it, mind your own business."

I thought again about that little girl. I remembered the way she avoided looking at me, the way she trembled as she hurried out of the store.

I hadn't helped her then.

"I think she needs my help," I said.

"What makes you say that?"

"Because of what you're not saying. I get the feeling she's a suspect."

He looked at the door, a classic "getaway" shifting of the eyes, and I knew I was right. Even though Angelina had supposedly been in Mexico when her family had been murdered, she was being considered a suspect.

While I sucked back noodles, a case was being built against her.

"But she was in Acapulco," I said.

"Penelope, let it go. I can't talk about this anymore."

I knew better than to press him. He hadn't told me anything, hadn't shared any of the details I'd hoped to gather, and yet he'd told me the thing I most needed to know.

Angelina Salvaggi needed my help. Again.

***

The family phone number was listed, but rang without being answered. I guessed it would be too hard for her to stay there, after everything that had happened. More likely she was staying with her boyfriend, Kevin McNeil, but there were too many McNeils listed in the City Directory.

The paper said Angelina worked at an optometrist's office on St. Clair. I narrowed it down to three with easy streetcar access, and found her working reception at the first one, within walking distance of the store on Wayburn.

She greeted me immediately, with only a hint of a smile.

At twenty-four, Angelina was now much taller than I was. In fact, she could have been a model, with her height, lean angles and general poise. High cheekbones and large dark eyes decorated a classic Roman face.

Still, there was a softness about her, despite her slender features.

"Are you Angelina Salvaggi?" I asked.

She looked alarmed, and for a moment I thought she might run away.

"Do I know you?" she asked.

"We used to be neighbors," I said.

"Then you knew my family."

"I did. I'm so sorry to hear about your tragedy."

"Thank you."

When she looked away, I realized she took me for a curiosity-seeker, so I thought I'd better pretend to buy some glasses. In fact, my eyesight is perfect.

"I need some good quality sunglasses. Can you recommend a brand?"

"Your face is small," she said without looking at me.

"Yes. I don't like when the frames are too wide."

"I think I might have something for you."

She went into the back. I thought again about that storage area in the corner store, the one behind the coolers. I had to fight the urge to follow her.

She returned a few minutes later with a Chanel frame, perfectly suited to my face. The kind of thing I'd never wear. Too expensive. Far too tasteful for me.

"It's perfect," I said. I looked at the price – $450. Kept a straight face.

"It comes with the case," she said.

"Good." For a moment there, I thought I might not be getting much of a bargain. But hey, it came with the case.

"Is that all you need?"

"Yes." I pulled out my Visa, hoping and not hoping it would clear.

It did.

"Have a good day," she said.

"Angelina, take my card. I'm a private investigator. If you need anything, give me a call. No charge. I'd like to help a neighbor."

She looked startled. I instantly regretted my boldness. However, as my Aunt Rachel would point out, it's part of me, for better or worse.

In any event, she allowed me to press the card into her open hand.

I think she said 'Thank you', but it was hard to be sure. She was already turning away, and her voice tripped on a sob.

***

Some good deeds are totally selfless. Others, less so.

I'm afraid this one was largely about how it made me feel, and not so much about what I could or couldn't do to help Angelina Salvaggi.

I didn't hear from her for weeks, but during that time I had the sense of a wrong being righted. As if at least one black mark had been removed from my personal ledger of deeds.

By the time she called, I hardly thought about her anymore. My conscience felt absolved, and therefore cleared.

So it was a surprise to hear her voice on the other end of the line.

"Is this Miss Canon?"

"Please, call me Penelope."

I waited. It's a trick I learned awhile back. Don't prompt the caller. Let her tell you the reason for the call.

The seconds seemed to stretch, but finally she said, "I need your help."

We met at a Panzerotti place on St. Clair, near where she worked.

She told me the story leading up to her trip to Mexico. Her parents had been against it. They were a Catholic family with strong ties to the neighborhood Church. They felt Angelina would hurt her reputation by going off with her boyfriend.

"Our last words were angry," she said. "I felt they never let me have any fun. Now I can't stop thinking about it. I loved them, you know."

Guilt. Something I could relate to. If possible, I felt even more sympathetic to Angelina knowing she had regrets of her own to live with.

"We all say and do things we're sorry for. No one would think you didn't love them, just because you had an argument. The timing is unfortunate, but...."

"The police think I arranged it all."

The words were dispatched without inflection, emotionless. Even her voice sounded disconnected, like the electronic voice that tells you the subway doors are about to close.

I looked at her, a thought worming its way into my mind. I tried to stomp on it, but it squirmed anyway.

Never being one for subtlety, I said, "Why do they think that? I mean, you were out of town."

She thought for a moment, and when she spoke her voice was back to its usual soft, sad timbre.

"I'm not sure why. But I could tell they thought so. They questioned both me and Kevin. They went easy on him, but when it came to me they were pretty harsh."

"What do you need me to do?"

"Well, I was hoping you could ask some questions around the neighborhood. I don't think Kevin or I should be seen doing that. But you could. You never know – maybe you'll find out who did this to my family."

"So we could bring the killer to justice."

"That's right. And clear my name. So the police will know it wasn't me."

She moved her folded pizza around on her plate.

"I have money," she added.

"I wouldn't charge you."

"That's very kind."

She met my eyes directly then, for perhaps the first time, as if trying to study my motivations.

"I remember you," she said slowly.

"From the store."

"Yes."

Something about her eyes told me she remembered not only me, but that day as well. And that she understood, at last, why I felt I owed her.

"So you'll help me?"

"I'll do my best."

But I already wondered how much help I'd be to her. Something felt wrong about the whole thing.

Why would the police suspect a grieving young woman who'd been out of town at the time of the murders?

She didn't look like an addict, didn't behave as if she had no morals.

She was a nice girl, to all appearances – raised on Holy Wafers and family.

My early sojourns to the neighborhood were unproductive. Everyone was horrified about the home invasion that had occurred in their midst. People were watchful, suspecting each other.

The community threw its support behind the sad young woman who'd lost her family.

The third time I rode my bike to Wayburn, I parked it outside our old house and walked up the street to the store. The sign still said Salvaggi's Convenience, but it needed fresh paint.

A group of teenagers were smoking in the small lot beside the store. They looked like young people in any urban centre – lean and mildly intimidating – but I knew from experience these were good kids. They snuck a smoke around the corner from time to time, but didn't dare get up to any great mischief, aware of being watched by neighborhood Nonnas who knitted on porches up and down the streets.

On a whim, and feeling youthful in my skimpy leather bomber jacket and biking boots, I decided to join them.

I pulled out my card by way of introduction, handing it to the biggest boy.

"My name's Penelope Canon. I'm investigating the crime that took place here a couple of months ago."

"You're a Private Eye," he said, handing my card to the next kid. "Cool."

"Do you guys hang here often?"

A general shifting of eyes and shuffling of feet.

"Sometimes. Not all the time."

"What about on March 10th. That was a Saturday."

"Yeah. We were here. But we didn't see anyone strange. We talked about it afterward. Nothing happened while we were here."

"What time did you stay till?"

"The store closes at 9:30. We usually hang till around 10."

"But that was a Saturday," another boy said. "We stayed till 10:30."

"That's right."

"Did you see anyone in the family that day?"

"Just the father. He was working the store. We went in for pop around 9."

"Did he seem normal?"

"Yeah. He was his usual self. A real nice guy. The whole thing really sucked."

"Did the police question any of you?"

The five boys looked at each other before shaking their heads. The big guy said, "Nah. We didn't see anything that would help. Otherwise we'd've told them."

"What about the daughter?" I let that hang, allowing them to interpret the deliberately vague question however they chose.

More shuffling of feet.

"She was in Mexico," one of the boys said.

"With her Inglese boyfriend," another added.

One of the boys snorted.

"What do you think of him?" I asked. I was taking this purely on instinct.

"Her father didn't like him, that's for sure."

"Neither did her brother."

"Had they been seeing each other long?"

"Nope. Only since she dumped Jimmy right around Christmas time."

Wait a minute. Jimmy?

"Who's Jimmy?"

"Jimmy Leone. He was engaged to Angelina for three years. Then she dumped him and started going out with the English prick."

"How'd he take it? Was there any bad blood between them?" This was getting interesting.

"Like a lamb," the oldest boy said. "He never made any trouble. Anyway, her family and his were close. They pushed her to get back together with him."

"She didn't deserve him," the only girl in the group said.

"Jimmy's a saint."

I thought it might be a good idea to track down Mr. Leone.

***

Jimmy Leone pulled a deck chair off the stack and placed it near his own – too close for comfort. I moved it a few feet away before sitting.

I looked up in time to see a hint of a smile.

He was full of muscle and energy. Blue eyes couldn't help their sparkle, despite the circumstances of our meeting.

I would not have described him as a saint.

A god, perhaps, but not a saint.

The kind of guy who could sell corn to farmers in Kansas. So long as they were women.

He looked to be around twenty-eight, only a few years younger than me. A fact that wasn't lost on me.

"They tell me you and Angelina were engaged." I threw that out with my usual subtlety.

"By-gones. Still, I feel bad for her. She didn't deserve that."

I studied his face, the perfect blend of sorrow and regret.

"Have you seen her since you broke up?"

"Once in a while we'll bump into each other. In the neighborhood. Other than that, no. We've talked a couple of times on the phone. I saw her at the funeral."

"So you'd say you're still friends?"

"Yeah, I'd say so. Like I said, I felt badly for her."

"You seem like a nice guy, Jim. Why'd she dump you?"

His eyes turned cold. "We went our separate ways."

"I heard she dumped you for another guy," I persisted. "Some English prick."

"Hey, it's her decision. And anyway, I wouldn't call him a prick."

"What would you call him?"

The smile returned. "I don't know. Maybe a *sciocco*."

I wracked my brain for my half-remembered Italian phrases from when I lived in Little Italy.

"A fool. Why?"

"Because he doesn't see it coming."

"Like you didn't see it coming?"

"Maybe."

The porch door opened and a middle-aged lady stepped out. She saw me and decided, out of politeness, to use English.

"Jimmy," she said, "Angelina just called."

"Ok, ok, I'll be right in." He looked alarmed, as if this was an unexpected revelation he would have preferred to avoid.

"No need to get up. She said to tell you she'd be here around 6 as usual."

As usual? What did that mean?

And suddenly it hit me. Just like that.

"She's leaving Kevin, isn't she? That's what you meant by *sciocco*. You and Angelina are getting back together."

He waved a hand, as if the answer was irrelevant. "Our families were friends, that's all. Anyway, you'll have to excuse me." He stood, his patience having reached its limit.

"Did it ever occur to you, Jimmy, that maybe Angelina has a thing for *scioccos*?"

"Get the hell out of here!"

"I'm going, Jimmy. But just so you know, I think you've been played, just like Kevin."

I turned to go, was about to plant my foot on the first veranda stair when I felt more than saw him lunge toward me.

Just in time, I jumped off the veranda, my ankle twisting slightly, but protected by the sturdy leather boot. In that instant I avoided his grasp.

I knew I couldn't outrun him, but tried anyway. Within seconds he would reach me, but I had to give it a shot.

As he grabbed my forearm, I spotted the group of teenagers on a porch across the street.

"Hey guys!" I called out.

"Penelope, how's it going?" the biggest kid said.

"Not so good. I need you guys to walk me to my bike."

Before he let go of me, Jimmy turned me to face him.

"We're not done," he said. His charming mask was gone, and in its place was the real face of Jimmy Leone, the lion, the hunter, the man of rage who'd slaughtered the Salvaggi family in cold blood.

Why?

Because she'd asked him to. Angelina, the angel of death. The little girl who despised her family with cause, with an unrelenting hatred. The woman bent on destruction.

"You are, Jimmy. You and Angelina. You're both done."

He released his grip and strode back to his house, to his mother, to the life he'd thrown away.

The kids walked me to my bike, smoking and laughing, innocent of knowledge.

But I knew. And I could never again pretend I didn't.

***

My Aunt Rachel has a saying: It'll all come out in the wash. And so it did, in its own way.

Angelina could have carried it to her grave, but Jimmy was not made of such stern stuff. His temper got the better of him under close questioning by Toronto's homicide detectives, and the truth came barreling out.

Angelina hated her father. By extension, she hated her mother and brother as well. She could never be free, as long as they were alive.

They had millions in savings squirreled away, and wouldn't part with it. They wouldn't even consider helping their daughter get a good start in married life.

All she'd asked for was enough to make a down payment on her own house, a house she and Jimmy could share.

The old bastard was as tight-fisted as he was perverted.

Then she came up with a plan.

She and Jimmy pretended to be through. She took up with Kevin, the Inglese idiota, and a few months later planned a trip to Mexico with him.

This was to be her alibi.

Meanwhile, Saint Jimmy was known throughout the neighborhood to have taken the breakup "like a lamb". His own good nature was his alibi.

Sometime after 2 am, he called the Salvaggi home to say he'd heard from Kevin about an emergency situation in Mexico involving Angelina. Mrs. Salvaggi was frantic. Jimmy promised to come right over and tell them the news in person.

They let him into their home without hesitation.

The lion in lamb's clothing.

A HAPPY CUSTOMER

I woke to the sound of an engine humming. Or maybe the noise was inside my head. It was muffled and I couldn't be sure.

My eyes were gummy and slow to open. A throbbing at the back of my skull reminded me of the night before.

The images were foggy, dispersing as quickly as they formed in the hangover haze of my memory.

At least I was alone. To all appearances, I'd spent the night that way. Small mercies....

As morbid as it might seem under the circumstances, my mind toyed with the question of my rather tenuous mortality. I seemed to have a penchant for brushing up against death. Too often I'd swaggered through 'the valley'. One of these days, the shadow was gonna get me.

It should have laid its claim the night Mom died. I remembered the accident with regrettable clarity.

She was drunk, of course, my mother. There'd been a fight with her boyfriend.

I was a wee bit-of-a-thing when it happened, only five years old. My brother Dale was ten. Being older, he got to sit in the front with Mom.

"Stop whining, Penelope," she said, buckling me into the child seat. I hadn't outgrown the contraption, but it hurt my pride being strapped into it like a baby.

I didn't see the truck, though I was blinded by its headlights. I heard my brother Dale's last word. More of a holler, really: *"Mom!"*

And then the crash.

They hunted for my father, but couldn't locate him. No big surprise there. Aunt Rachel saved me from the orphanage. For that I'll always be grateful.

She was an odd duck, my mother's sister. She tried her best, in her eccentric way, to raise me right. I suspect my 'angry teen years' were more than she'd bargained for.

I doubt she was very sorry when, at eighteen, I ran off and got married.

I tried not to think about Bruce. Memories of my ex-husband made my head pound, and for a moment I worried I might have an aneurysm.

We weren't together long, Bruce and I. Like most young women who carry a big rage, my anger was mostly self-directed. His, though, presented itself in outward physical aggression.

The night he strangled me till stars ruptured behind my eyes, I knew I'd reached a pivotal moment.

Like most epiphanies, this one came down to a single choice: either put away my anger once and for all, or let it finish me. Let *it* put *me* away.

So I left Bruce and took back my maiden name, Penelope Canon. I got on with the business of living.

I'm still alive. Still angry, sometimes, but not with that wild, destructive rage I used to have.

Not usually.

Still living dangerously, though. I'd have to work on that.

Rolling over, I accepted the pain at the back of my head. It wasn't an injury — for that I was thankful. It was just a reaction to whatever I'd consumed the night before.

'Acceptance' is the key to life, in my opinion. With acceptance, all things, even a blasting headache, are manageable.

I was still dressed. That was something else to be grateful for. It wouldn't be cool to wake up naked feeling this badly.

I reached down to my skinny jeans, working my fingers into the right-front pocket. My keychain was there, digging into my thigh.

I drew it out, snagging a thread.

It took some effort, but I pried my tiny pocket-knife open and used it to cut the duct tape from my wrists and ankles.

Images from the previous day flooded my mind.

I'd met with a client, Bob Regent, for lunch. He wanted me to track down a crooked investment broker who'd absconded with half-a-million of his life's savings.

I explained to Bob that finding these guys was one thing – they often used a string of aliases and had a variety of financial wells from which to draw – but recovering losses was something else.

I hate taking jobs where the chances of success are slim. Often the clients have unrealistic expectations. When all is said and done, they'll sometimes blame me for a less-than-stellar outcome.

Bob assured me he understood. He wanted to find the son of a bitch, even if he couldn`t recover his lost money, and he was happy to pay my usual fee to do it.

Well, as they say, Kitty needs a new pack of Whiskas, so I took the job. Of course, I warned Bob one more time it might take weeks, even months, to get a bead on the so-called "Jeff Winger". Con-men are the hardest crooks to nail. Their entire make-up is based on a structure of lies.

"Penelope," he said, "just do your best."

Bob gave me what information he could – a list of known associates and a handful of places Winger had frequented during their dealings.

Little did I know the first lead I followed up on would turn out to be the money-maker. Sometimes that happens.

Not often.

It was just a name: Jim Stalwart. Bob had never met the guy, but he'd heard Jeff Winger mention him.

Bob recalled hearing that Stalwart worked for a downtown law firm, Dohmish and Gray.

He was right. I called D&G and was put through to Stalwart on the first try.

Jim Stalwart was happy to talk to me. When I told him, without going into details, that I was trying to locate Jeff Winger, he could hardly contain his excitement.

"I didn't catch your name," he said.

"Penelope Canon," I replied.

"Ms. Canon, you couldn't have called at a better time."

He admitted he had his own axe to grind – he'd lost a whack of dough to Winger, about 80 thou – and wondered whether he could piggy-back on my client's investigation.

I told Jim Stalwart I'd be happy to help him, but he'd have to cover my fee independently of my first client. It wouldn't be fair to foist the bill onto one customer while working for two.

Stalwart agreed.

He suggested we meet so he could sign my contract. He promised to bring any info he thought might help with the search.

"I'm not far from your office now," I said. "Would you like me to drop by?"

"Not here. I'm meeting a client this afternoon, but I'll finish at 5. Let's grab a bite."

At 5:30 I sauntered, skinny jeans and all, into Scotland Yard, a fine and funky pub on The Esplanade.

Jim Stalwart was already there, watching the door from a booth to my left. He spotted the snug black bomber jacket and red poppy I told him I'd be wearing. He flagged me down.

I gave him the same spiel I'd given Bob – there was no guarantee of finding the elusive con-man Winger and even less chance of recovering financial losses. Like Bob, Jim Stalwart was determined to bring Winger to justice.

Stalwart had been saving to care for his aging mother. On a day-to-day basis, the loss wouldn't break him, but it was a hit that pissed him off, just the same. He was willing to pay my meagre fee with no guarantee of success.

It was the *principle* of the thing.

By the time my curried chicken arrived, I'd given Stalwart – Jim – a good look-over. He wasn't my usual type, but then, I hadn't had much luck with my relationships in the past.

It might be time for me to find a new 'type'.

Jim was handsome, though not in the classical sense. Brow a bit too wide, nose not quite centered on his face.

Symmetry off just a smidge, but not enough to hurt the eyes.

He was certainly well dressed. Clean casual.

I looked down at my worn-out jeans and the too-tight purple sweater that was pilling from the wash. My boots were scuffed and my hair was more of a 'mane' than a fashion statement. As usual, I wasn't wearing jewelry, and my only nod to conventional fashion was the poppy I wore this time of year.

By comparison, Jim was downright natty.

But what the hell, I could clean up nicely, too, given the right occasion.

Anyway, I never date clients, so the chemistry between us, if I wasn't imagining it, would have to wait. I let him order a drink for both of us and cut a path to the ladies' room. I studied my reflection, doing my best to repair my disheveled 'Sydney Carton' image using the tools I'd had the foresight to shove into my pocket – namely a comb and a half-squashed tube of lipstick.

Great color, though. It couldn't hurt.

When I got back to the table, Jim handed me a napkin on which he'd jotted down five names. I didn't say so, but three of them were already on the list Bob had given me. Jim's list, though, included phone numbers for two of the names.

I folded the napkin and wedged it into my left pocket to keep the tube of lipstick company. My keys were, as usual, threatening to wear a hole in my right pocket. Or into my thigh.

"Thanks for the Intel," I said.

"My pleasure."

He pointed at my glass, but I shook my head. I didn't need another drink. I'd barely touched the first.

Jim Stalwart didn't have much to offer in terms of info on our con-man. His association with Winger was brief, but his description of the bearded financial manager was in line with Bob's.

He signed my contract, paying my retainer in cash.

The waiter took away my half-eaten plate of curry. I sipped my drink, sensing Jim's attention was waning.

"Let me get the bill," I said. "I can expense it, since you're a client."

"Thank you," he said. "I'll be right back."

Jim made his way to the men's room as I handed the waiter my plastic.

I wanted to call it a night, so I finished my drink before he returned.

By the time he got back, I was pulling on my jacket. The poppy had come loose. Not wanting to damage the worn leather, I'd stuck it into the wool lining on the lapel. I should have anchored it with a bit of rubber.

Jim reached for his coat. His poppy needed no adjustment. Like his hair, clothes... hell, like the man himself, the poppy was perfectly turned out.

"Do you need a lift?" he asked.

"No. I don't have far to go."

It was a cool November, and the sun set early in our part of the hemisphere. Evenings were downright cold.

I zipped my inadequate jacket all the way up.

The drug didn't take effect till we were on the sidewalk. At first it felt as if the single shot of rum was taking hold. By the time the pub door shut behind us, my head was spinning out of control.

"Are you all right?" he said.

Jim. That was his name. Jim...Stalwart. I fought to remember.

"What the fuck did you do?" I said, pushing him away.

I staggered, trying to get someone, anyone, to stop and help, but given the way I was dressed, like some throw-away street kid, and with my speech slurred, staggering hopelessly, I didn't present a credible sight.

A burly young man reached out for my arm.

"Do you need help?" he asked.

Jim explained that I was ok.

"Just too much to drink," Jim said.

The man nodded and went on his way.

I don't remember getting into Jim's car.

It was early, only 6:30 or 7, but already dark. I recall only snatches of the rest of the evening – Jim pulling me from the car, warning me not to vomit on the seat. He was almost gentle, holding my thick hair as I leaned over the toilet once we were inside.

Thank God I hadn't finished my curry. As it was, the spicy chicken burned my throat on the way back up.

I have a memory of Jim talking quietly as he wrapped duct tape around my wrists, but I'm not sure what he said.

I do remember him repeating my name, Penelope, rolling it off his tongue the way a lover would.

I didn't mind. I let the sound of his voice lull me into sleep.

He'd left me bound on the couch in his basement. At one point he'd taped my mouth, but I guess he was afraid I'd gag and choke on my vomit.

Good to know he didn't plan to kill me. Something else to be thankful for.

***

I looked around.

It was daylight. There were windows in what must be a basement, but they were high and small.

Still, I was petite and capable of climbing. I flexed my muscles, stretching to free the circulation before trying to get up.

My head throbbed, but not as badly as before.

I took my time, wiggling toes and fingers under the horse-hair blanket Jim had used to cover me.

Before I could sit up, the sound of footsteps warned me Jim was back.

If that was his name.

Damn!

I shut my eyes and let my jaw go slack, possum-like.

"Still asleep?" he said. "You must need to use the bathroom. I brought coffee. It'll help with the headache."

There was no point keeping up the charade. Anyway, I needed to pee.

I opened my eyes. "What did you do to me?"

"You're not hurt. A few hours' sleep will take care of the hangover."

He replaced the tape he'd removed from my mouth with a new piece.

"Don't try to get up too quickly," he said. "I'll help you. I don't want you to hurt yourself."

Big of you, I thought, but could only mumble behind the tape.

Jim reached for the blanket.

I had to think fast. Which was a problem, since my mind was set to *slow-mo*.

Once Jim pulled the blanket off me he'd realize I was still holding my pocket-knife. It wasn't much of a dagger, but the self-defense class I'd taken would come in handy.

'Surprise' is a girl's best weapon.

Surprise, and a mean right hook.

The blanket came off gently.

"Careful, now," Jim said, reaching to help me.

I sprang to my feet, pushing him off balance. With both hands wrapped around the pocket-knife, I raised it and stabbed, allowing the full force of my rage to guide the tiny blade to his left eye.

He shrieked, but the injury wasn't deep. It would only slow him down, not stop him. Fighting to keep my balance, I brought one scuffed boot up and plowed it into his groin.

Jim went down hard.

Even that wouldn't stop him. He was a big man, and physically fit. I, on the other hand, was still the pipsqueak I'd been when my mother strapped me into that child seat so many years ago.

I'd have to make sure Jim stayed down.

Looking around, I saw a heavy ornament, a china cat of all things, on the table beside the couch.

I grabbed it and slammed it against his head, more than once, I'm ashamed to say.

Then I ripped the tape off my mouth.

Before staggering away to get help, I couldn't resist a parting shot.

"Not today, you son of a bitch. You don't have what it takes to finish me."

My bravado was wasted on the unconscious con-man, and my speech was slurred anyway.

Still, it felt good to have the last word.

From that point on my memory gets shaky. I was running on adrenalin and it carried me out of Jim's house. I didn't know what time it was, but it seemed to be morning rush hour. I flagged down a passing car and convinced the driver, a middle-aged man, to use his cell-phone to call the cops.

When the police arrived, they found 3 million in cash stuffed into a carry-on bag beside Jim's front door, along with a single suitcase. A bus ticket in his pocket told us he'd planned a trip to Miami that afternoon.

He would have known better than to fly into the U.S. carrying a bag of cash, with the airport security in place these days. He'd take the bus, just one more snow-bird in search of sunshine.

Once he arrived in the 'land of sand', he'd pop the money into a number of off-shore accounts, then book a flight to anywhere.

He must have damn nearly pissed himself when I telephoned, asking questions about "Mr. Winger".

And, speaking of peeing... I did a rain dance at 52 Division. The receptionist pointed to the ladies' room, where I avoided looking into the mirror as I washed my hands.

I ran my comb through matted hair and straightened my poppy, which had miraculously survived the ordeal. Still keeping my eyes averted from the mirror, I splashed cold water on my face. I used scratchy paper towels to dry, hoping to scour away at least one layer of grime.

I couldn't wait to call my real client, Bob Regent. My head was still pounding, but my tongue was not as swollen as it had been. I'd be able to talk without slurring my words, and that was one conversation I was looking forward to.

After all, there's nothing like a happy customer.

THE 14th OF FOREVER

"I'm just saying, as pagan fertility festivals go, this one really sucks."

"You wouldn't feel that way if you were dating."

"Maybe not," Mallory, said, "but on behalf of all the single guys and gals, I think we could do without the fat cherub and his nasty red arrows. Anyway, what are you and Celia doing tonight?"

It was only half a beat. No one else would have noticed, but Mallory knew him. She sensed a stiffening of Jerome's shoulders when he answered.

"Lucky me," he said, "I get to save my money this year. Celia's out of town, staying with her mom in Cornwall."

"And the kids?"

"They went with her. We figured at their ages it wouldn't hurt them to miss a week of school."

Jerome crept onto the shoulder, planting the cherry on the Crown Vic's roof. Daytime traffic was a bitch on the 401, especially given the winter conditions, and cops were an easy target for rush-hour motorists. He took his sweet time exiting the vehicle.

The scene had been cordoned off with pylons, funneling westbound traffic to the left. The victim had politely fallen onto the far right westbound collectors' lane. That meant they didn't have to shut down all four lanes, but the right one and on-ramp were a bust.

The drop from the Don Mills overpass wasn't overly dramatic. She'd initially bounced off the roof of a 2008 Grand Caravan. She might have even survived, except for her frailty…and the Ford Escape that caught her on the rebound.

A Uniform waved as they approached.

"I'm Detective Mallory Tosh, and this is my partner Detective Jerome Christie."

The constable flashed a crooked grin. "Tim Beckwith. Nice to meet you, Detective." He nodded at Jerome. "What's happening, Chris?"

Chris was Jerome's nickname, a handle he detested. He smiled at the constable.

"Same old, Tim. How's our victim?"

"Still quite dead."

Jerome chuckled and Mallory rolled her eyes at the constable's bit of gallows humor.

It might have looked like a simple traffic accident, but in Toronto all "sudden deaths" are first handed off to Homicide. Only when foul play is ruled out and the death signed off by the city Coroner as fully explained can the case be closed.

"Bad time of day for it," Mallory said, nodding at the bottleneck that had already formed under the Don Mills bridge.

"Shit, Mal," Jerome said, "is there ever a good time of day to end up like that?"

The forensic photographer was hard at it, recording the bundle of fabric and blood from every available angle.

Crime lab techies in bunny suits, shod in white-paper booties, combed two and a half lanes for any evidence of wrongdoing.

"Jumper?" Mallory said.

"Looks like," Jerome nodded.

"I told you, my friend. People really don't like Valentine's Day."

***

Sherman Grady was not your Joe-average accountant. Despite his well-known dexterity with numbers, he harbored a romantic soul.

He replaced the receiver, having confirmed the flowers would be delivered to his wife by noon. The accompanying note would read: *Yours till the 14th of Forever.*

Next, he made sure their reservation was secured for 6:30 at the David Duncan House. He'd booked it months in advance, knowing how difficult it was to nab a table anyplace decent on Valentine's Day.

His mind was not operating at its usual capacity lately, so he felt better having nailed down the plans.

He thought back to his wedding, 30 years ago today. She'd been a stunning bride, a rare blend of beauty and modesty, confidence and poise. Long blonde hair that fell in natural honey-colored waves over ivory shoulders.

Sherman had been a handsome enough young man in his own right – arrow-straight bearing and a quick smile. He knew how lucky he'd been, how his charm had come to his aid in winning her undying love.

They'd sworn it then, and his promise was as meaningful today as it had been on Valentine's Day 30 years ago.

Yours till the 14th of Forever...

Sherman wasn't given to displays of emotion, at least not outwardly. He liked to think he carried himself with professional grace. Certainly, it stood him well in the current corporate climate, with colleagues running around in a constant state of suppressed panic, everyone watching the heads roll and doing the math...

Life, he thought, *is a game of chicken. When you see that proverbial light at the end of every tunnel, you've got to stare it down and pray it's not an oncoming freight train.*

He was good at that, good at maintaining an aura of quiet calm in the face of chaos. It was this quality that had helped him stay employed these past 30 years and still kept him in professional demand.

When he'd asked for her hand, he'd told her he would provide, that he would keep a steady job, and he had, despite the corporate shenanigans and shake-ups.

He'd done it by coupling an analytical mind, exceptional business skills, a computer-like genius for math with a warm smile and undeniable charm.

Despite his normally cool demeanor, he couldn't help but raise an eyebrow when his phone rang and the call display showed the extension for Human Resources.

"Hi, Judy," he said. "What can I do for you?"

It might have been anything. Five of his coworkers had been packaged off the previous week. As the company's only accountant, he'd felt relatively safe, especially since he reported directly to the CEO, but one never really knew.

"Sherm," she said, an edge of nervousness in her voice, "can you come to my office?"

"Of course, Judy. What's up?"

"Just come here, Sherman, right away, please."

Stay calm, he told himself.

He made his way down the hall, past the empty boardroom. It reminded him of the old joke: *How do you create a successful small business? Well, first you start with a big business…Ha-ha!*

The elegant boardroom used to be nearly impossible to book, being used daily for back-to-back meetings by every department.

These days though, it seemed the only meetings held with any regularity were the ones in Judy's office – the ones where the final handshake took place.

Sherman peeked into Thomas' office on his way down the hall.

"Still on for lunch?" Tom asked.

"Still on," Sherman agreed. "Can't chat, though. I'm off to a meeting with Judy."

"Oh, cripes," Tom said. "Well, good luck!" Then, as an afterthought, he added, "Been nice knowing ya!"

Sherman chuckled, more to calm his own nerves than because the joke was funny.

The door to Judy's office was closed. He knocked before opening it.

"Come in, Sherm," she said. "Have a seat."

He looked around the room at the unfamiliar faces.

Instead of sitting, he asked, "Judy, what's happening?" He wasn't jittery, exactly – his professionalism wouldn't allow for that – but he was noticeably anxious.

Judy stood and came around the desk.

"Sherm," she said, taking his elbow and guiding him to a seat at the round table before settling down beside him, "these are Detectives Mallory Tosh and Jerome Christie of the Toronto Metro Police Services. Please, Detectives, sit down." She waved at the empty chairs.

Mallory threw a look at her partner. Out of respect, it was usual to stand to deliver unfortunate news, but the silly HR person had positioned it so they didn't have much choice.

Mallory nodded, and she and Jerome sat across from Sherman Grady.

"Mr. Grady," Mal began, "we're here about…."

"Oh, my God," Sherman sputtered, "is it Valerie? Has something happened to Valerie?"

Sherman was, after all, good at math. He and Valerie had no children, no other close family members or dependents. Valerie had not been herself this past year. She'd been showing signs of early-onset dementia. Since her 55th birthday last year, she'd taken medical leave from her job at the bank, citing "stress" as the underlying condition.

And it was stressful for her, to find herself losing her ability to handle numbers quickly and efficiently, and subsequently coming under the scrutiny of the bank's management.

He'd taken her to the family doctor, who'd prescribed a cholinesterase inhibitor and a mild dose of memantine to minimize the memory loss and confusion.

Most days weren't too bad, but lately she'd begun leaving the house after he did in the morning. If he couldn't reach her on the home phone, he'd usually get her on her cell, but sometimes she'd forget to put it into her pocket.

Just last week, on Wednesday, she'd called him from the supermarket. She couldn't remember why she'd gone there, and was panicking. He'd had to take a time-out from his spreadsheets to pick her up and drive her home.

The doctor had her lined up for testing at the Memory Facility in North York, but that was still a month away.

Jerome flashed a look at Mallory.

She understood, and let him take the lead.

"Why do you say that, Mr. Grady?" he asked.

It might seem unkind, but they couldn't let it pass. After all, every sudden death was considered questionable until they had ruled out the possibility of foul play.

Grady had immediately assumed something had happened to his wife. The detectives didn't know him. They weren't aware of his lack of other family, his wife's medical history or his proficiency at math.

For all they knew, he might have a much darker reason for suspecting "something" had happened to Valerie.

"She…she hasn't been herself lately. She's been…easily confused." Sherman fought to regain his composure.

"Sherm," Judy said, taking his hand, "I'm so sorry."

Mallory shot a look at the HR manager that said "Stand down, lady."

"I'll let you three talk privately," Judy said. "I'll be in the break room if you need me, Sherman."

When the door had closed behind Judy, Mallory spoke.

"In what way has your wife been confused?"

"I can't really explain it," Sherman said. "She used to be so sharp. Lately she doesn't always know what day it is. I had to remind her yesterday that today is our anniversary. We were married on Valentine's Day and we always celebrate with a nice dinner. She used to get excited, but now she doesn't remember."

"When did you last see your wife?" Jerome asked.

"This morning, when I left for work. Around 7:00. Please, tell me what's happened."

Mallory studied Grady's face, taking in the guarded but growing panic.

"We're sorry to tell you, Mr. Grady," she said, "but your wife has been involved in an accident."

"What?" Sherman said, rising to his feet. "What happened? Is she all right? I have to get to her. Where is she?"

"Please, sit down, Mr. Grady," Jerome said. "Mrs. Grady, at least we believe it's Mrs. Grady, died this morning in a traffic accident. It happened around 7:15."

"But you're not sure it's Valerie?" Sherman said, his voice registering hope.

"We're fairly certain it's her, Mr. Grady," Mallory said.

Sherman thought once again of his wedding day, 30 years earlier. Although he struggled for composure, he was unable to stem the tears that threatened to spill from his eyes.

"I'll have to identify her," he said. "You'd better take me to her."

"Mr. Grady," Jerome said, his voice kind but firm, "it was a very bad accident. We'll be using her dental records to identify her. She's with the Coroner's Office now. I'm afraid you won't be able to see her till they release her to the funeral home."

"What do I do?"

Detectives Tosh and Christie had attended their share of grieving loved ones. They had broken the bad news more times than they could count.

It always came down to the same question: *What do I do now?*

What do I do this morning? This afternoon? This evening? Tomorrow?

It was the human fallback position, to take action, to fight the inevitable.

They always needed to be doing *something*.

It didn't matter that nothing they might do, no conceivable action on their part, would change the facts.

Their loved one was gone.

Death is final.

Just the same, for the living, it was important to be doing *something*.

"We'll need you to come down to the division with us," Mallory said. "You'll need to sign the requisition for the dental records. You'll need to identify her belongings – her coat, purse, clothing."

"She was carrying her purse?"

"Yes, sir," Jerome said.

"I'll tell Judy I'm leaving now," Sherman said. "She'll let my boss know."

"There's no need, Mr. Grady," Mallory said. "Ms. Hanover knows you'll be leaving with us, to identify the belongings."

***

Sherman stared at the coffeemaker in the visitors' lounge at 33 Division. He'd often seen the police cruisers driving on Don Mills or York Mills, on their way to their base on Upjohn, but he'd never been inside the building.

The two detectives had left him sitting there for what seemed like hours, but was probably closer to twenty minutes. Although he hadn't taken his eyes off that coffeepot for more than the quarter-second it took to blink, he could not have described it, nor, if pressed could he even have told you it was, in fact, a coffeepot.

It simply didn't register. It was there, in his sightline, but the image didn't penetrate via the optic nerve to travel to his brain.

It was just there.

And he was there.

This was really happening.

Twenty minutes, thirty, it hardly mattered. Time had no essence. It was merely something to be tolerated, passed through, withstood.

Of course, that could be said of many things in life.

They needed to be withstood.

Sherman could not have described his thoughts, as he sat there staring at the coffeepot, back arrow-straight, hands on his knees, a proper schoolboy waiting for instructions from his teacher.

His mind had somehow detached itself from his body. He had the eerie sense that he was watching himself, that the real Sherman was hovering somewhere near the ceiling lights, poised to fly away without notice, abandoning him in that strangely sterile room.

"Would you like a cup of coffee, Mr. Grady?"

It took a second before he realized she was speaking to him.

"Huh?" he said.

He turned to see Detective Mallory Tosh enter the room, followed by her partner, Christie. The detectives were carrying what appeared to be evidence bags.

Sherman's stomach churned as he recognized Valerie's winter coat. It had cost a small fortune – a birthday gift when she'd turned 55 late last year – but it was lovely. A stylish cashmere, with snug lining, perfect for Canadian winters, and a beautifully tapered cut that flared at the hips, enhancing her still regal figure.

Valerie had clapped her hands when she opened the box, and they were both astonished at how well he'd guessed her size and fit.

That had been months ago, back when his wife still clung to a semblance of mental normalcy.

"I wondered if you'd like a cup of coffee," Mallory repeated. "You were looking at the coffeepot."

"Oh," he said, "no, I didn't realize I was doing that. But yes, I guess I would appreciate a cup. That's very kind of you."

Mallory looked at Jerome, who raised a brow in acknowledgment. Neither would say it out loud, but they'd discussed it many times before, how the grief-stricken, the "loved ones", always seemed to follow a script. Their behavior might vary wildly from case to case, depending on their own unique personalities and experiences, but they each held onto a basket of words they could dip into during times of crisis.

Kind was one such word.

The deeper the grief, the more profound the shock, the more firmly the family member would cling to the notion of kindness in others.

"Not at all," Mallory said. "Let me get that for you." She passed the bag she was carrying to her partner.

"We have to ask you," Jerome said, "whether you recognize these items. Take your time. We need to leave them in the bags, but I'll put them here on the table. Please just look at each one. Let me know if you need me to turn the bags over."

"Yes." Sherman left the affirmation to rest on the ensuing silence.

The detectives allowed the gap to build, hoping for a follow-up comment from Grady.

When he did not elaborate, Jerome said, "Do you recognize any of these items?"

Mallory placed a ceramic mug in front of Sherman.

He lifted it to his mouth before answering.

"Yes," he repeated. "That's Valerie's coat. I'm sure of it. I bought it for her last fall. And that's her favorite purse – cream-colored to match the coat. Was she carrying her ID?"

"That's right, Mr. Grady," Mallory said gently. "That's how we knew to contact you. She had her ID in her purse, along with your office and cell phone numbers as an emergency contact."

Grady's perfect posture seemed to disintegrate before their eyes. He slumped in his chair, wrapping both hands around the hot mug for comfort.

"Oh, my God, it's really her. It's really Valerie, isn't it?"

"Yes," Jeremy said, "we're afraid so."

"Do you know why she might have been walking along Don Mills this morning?" Mallory asked.

"She's had a few of these episodes lately. Her dementia seems to be increasing. Last week she left the house and went to the supermarket, but came to her senses and called me on her cell. I picked her up and took her back home."

"But why Don Mills? Was it normal for her to walk there?"

"No. I don't think she's ever done that before. But I work near there. It's possible she was trying to get to my office."

"That would make sense," Jeremy said. "The accident happened at 7:17 this morning. That's a very short time after you left her at seven. Would she have been able to dress herself and walk to the Don Mills overpass in that short of a time?"

"Is that where it happened?" Sherman asked. "Did she fall from the bridge at the 401?"

"Mr. Grady," Mallory said, forcing him to meet her eyes, "she would not have fallen. There's no way anyone could fall from that overpass. The safety railing is too high."

Sherman digested the fact, struggling to avoid the obvious conclusion.

"Are you saying she…Are you saying… Did my wife jump off the bridge?"

"We can't say anything with certainty at this point," Jerome said. "We're just trying to nail down the timeline. Do you think Mrs. Grady – Valerie – do you think she could have walked to the overpass in the short time since you left her?"

"She was already dressed when I left," Sherman said. "Until last summer she still worked at the bank, the one at Don Mills and York Mills. She was a creature of routine – habit, if you like. Even though she was no longer able to work, due to her dementia, she still liked to get up with me in the morning, dress and have breakfast."

"You say she worked at the Don Mills and York Mills bank?" Mallory said. "Is it possible, Mr. Grady, that she thought she was walking to work?"

Sherman paused.

"Yes, that's certainly possible. We live…lived…I mean, our place is a condo in one of the high-rises at Sheppard. I usually take the car, and since she's been ill, I keep her keys with me. I used to drop her off at work every morning and pick her up at night, but it wouldn't be difficult for her to walk there."

"Was your wife well physically?" Jerome asked. "She looked frail to us, but of course, under the circumstances, it's hard to tell."

"Valerie has always been fit, and proud of her figure. The past few months, though, I think she sometimes forgets to eat. She has lost some weight. You could say she's been frailer than usual."

"Had your wife been diagnosed?" Mallory asked.

"Not yet. The family doctor prescribed a cognition-enhancing drug, and set up an appointment at the North York memory clinic. They had planned to assess her to see if the problem is...was Alzheimer's. The appointment was scheduled for April."

"Meanwhile, you were coping with the problem?"

"Yes. We were coping."

A young woman with a ponytail and a short tweed skirt came into the lounge area.

"Detectives," she said, "can I speak with you for a moment?"

Tosh and Christie followed the woman, leaving Sherman to once again study the coffeepot at 33 Division.

***

Some time later, the detectives returned. Christie carried a box of pastries, which he set on the table near Sherman.

"Mr. Grady," he said, "have a doughnut."

"No, thank you."

"Mr. Grady," Mallory said, "it's going to be a long day for you. Please, we insist, you need to eat something. If not a doughnut, then we'll have someone bring you a sandwich if you like."

Grady let out a sigh. "The doughnut will be okay," he said, but didn't reach for the box.

Mallory opened the lid. "What kind?"

Finally, Sherman chose an old-fashioned, chewing slowly and without tasting.

"Did your wife have any friends?" Jerome asked. "Was there anyone she remained in contact with socially, maybe someone she'd worked with at the bank?"

"What do you mean? Why do you ask? We have a few friends, like everyone. People we get together with occasionally for dinner or drinks."

"That's it? We've been trying to get a handle on her state of mind, whether she was depressed, whether she'd been considering harming herself."

Grady sat up straight in his chair.

"My wife," he said, "was a very sick woman. She wasn't well enough to engage in any kind of a social life. We maintained a few friendships together, but she didn't have the strength to see people without me."

"What about before," Mallory asked. "I mean before she got sick. While she was still working. Was there anyone she was close to then? Anyone she might still want to see?"

"You think she was trying to see a friend? Not coming to my office, but to her old workplace? I suppose that's possible. There was a lady...I can't remember...I think her name was Sheila. They used to have lunch together regularly."

Jerome nodded at Mallory. "Yes," he said. "That would be Sheila Matheson. We have someone speaking with her now."

The change in the room was barely perceptible. Mallory, though, picked up on it immediately. She'd been raised in a family where being sensitive to mood changes was a valuable survival skill.

Jerome sensed it too, but would have been hard-pressed to describe what exactly was different.

Sherman didn't bat an eye. He made no move, no comment. And yet the very air that surrounded him had become somehow charged – electrified – with a current of anxiety.

It lasted for less than a second. Sherman recovered, took a sip of his coffee, and said, "Yes, that's right. Sheila Matheson. That was her name."

"The reason we asked," Jerome said, "about Mrs. Grady's friends is because..." He paused.

Mallory picked up the sentence where he left off.

"A couple of passing motorists," she said, "reported seeing someone on the bridge with your wife."

"Of course they weren't sure," Jerome said. "They were heading east on the 401, at highway speed. Still, a handful have called in and said they saw a woman in a white coat, followed by a man dressed in either brown or black. They said it almost looked like they were together, even though he was a little behind her."

"A man?" Sherman said. "They must be mistaken. Why would Valerie be out walking with a man at that hour of the morning? Especially as sick as she was. It must have been a stranger. Someone who happened to be walking there at the same time."

"That's possible," Mallory said. "The only thing that seems odd is why a man would just keep going. Why wouldn't he stop and call 911 on his cell phone? Or flag down a passing driver to get help?"

"If I was walking behind a lady and saw her climb over that railing, I'd try to stop her," Jerome said. "If I couldn't stop her, then for sure I'd try to get help."

"Do you think someone pushed her over the railing?" Sherman said. "That's just crazy. Why would anyone want to hurt Valerie?"

"I'm sure it won't amount to anything," Mallory said. "It's just something we have to follow up. Besides," she added, "your wife might have waited for the man to pass before... Maybe he didn't know what she was about to do."

"But as far as you know," Jerome said, "your wife wasn't seeing any friends socially, I mean, without you present."

"No," Sherman said. "She really wasn't well enough for that."

"Very good," Mallory said. "Our people will ask around at the bank, but it looks like this was an accident resulting from early onset-dementia."

"Are you well enough to drive, Mr. Grady?" Jerome asked. "We can take you to your car, or if you like we can have someone chauffeur you home, and we can deliver your car for you."

"It's a short drive home from my office," Sherman said. "Please, take me to my car. I'll be okay."

"Is there anyone who can stay with you?" Mallory asked.

"No. But I'm really tired. I'll get some rest. There will be arrangements to make. When will my wife be released to the funeral home?"

"The autopsy should be completed by Wednesday. Unless we tell you differently, you'll be able to make arrangements any time after that."

Sherman nodded and drank the rest of his coffee.

"What am I going to do?" he asked, staring into the mug.

***

Home at last, Sherman poured himself a strong drink. He wasn't much of an imbiber, but the past five hours had left him knackered. He still had the feeling his soul was floating somewhere outside of his body, like he was disconnected from himself.

He fondled his wedding picture in its ornate frame and remembered once more how beautiful she had been, how much they had loved each other.

The sense of loss was nearly overwhelming.

***

Robert McQuade and Sheila Matheson sat together nervously in the visitors' lounge at 33 Division. They didn't speak – they didn't have to. They'd discussed the problem many times before. Each knew almost by heart the story they intended to tell.

***

Sherman nursed his drink. He hadn't slept the night before, and felt himself drifting into that sweet release, but forced himself to remain awake, at least a little longer.

Time was neither linear nor circular, in his experience. Instead, it was a game of hopscotch. Once you'd lived through a moment, you could relive it easily and at will.

Sometimes, though, time got the better of you. Sometimes it dragged you back and forth, hopping like a madman over the chalky pavement, reliving moments, days, weeks you would rather relegate to the past.

Recalling sights, smells, feelings you longed to forget.
Anything could act as a trigger for the game.
A particularly poignant piece of music.
The way a dress clung to a woman's hips.
Anything.

"Elizabeth," he said, for the hundredth time, cradling their wedding picture against his chest, the one with the heart-shaped wreath of red roses as a backdrop, "why did you have to die?"

Everything had gone to shit, the day they'd discovered she had stage four ovarian cancer. All of their sweet plans, their gilded dreams, blasted into the stratosphere in that horrible moment of clarity.

The children they would never have, the travel they would never enjoy. The old-age comfort they would never share.

How deep their love had been, even in that awful moment!

If he could have captured it, preserved it under glass, confined it to a spreadsheet – but it was nothing more than memory now.

Nothing more than a bitter-sweet mental album filled with images of a life that wasn't meant to be.

And oh, the grief! The grief that never seemed to end.

In his darkest hour he had turned in desperation to her sister, Valerie, who shared her figure, her honey-blond hair, her voice and physical beauty.

And Valerie, haunted by her own sorrow at her sister's death, had turned to him.

They'd married, as had he and Elizabeth, on Valentine's Day, a tribute to his sense of romance and his commitment to finding happiness beyond grief.

It seemed, at the time, the best solution for both of them, to pick up the lost threads of love and use them to forge a new love, a new life.

After all, they'd known each other for years. It seemed to make sense.

After mere months, Sherman realized his mistake.

Valerie may have *looked* like Elizabeth, but that was where the resemblance ended.

Where Elizabeth was modest, elegant and poised, Valerie was demanding, impossible to please, at times almost a hateful shrew.

She belittled him, mocked his source of livelihood, his love of numbers, his lack of interest in earning more money.

Her job at the bank paid slightly more than his and she never let him forget it.

The final insult, though, had come early last year, when he discovered she'd been having an affair.

Out of respect for his own beloved Elizabeth, and knowing he was doomed to never find a love like that again, he'd remained wedded to her sister those past 20 years. He'd used every ounce of his outward calm, his charm and wit to hold that marriage together, despite her insults, her sudden bursts of rage, her appetite for material things.

But an affair?

That was simply too much.

Sherman valued fidelity and trust above all things.

That was what made him such an exceptional accountant.

He found out the truth quite by accident, that Valerie had been stepping out with a coworker by the name of Robert McQuade. He was at a local restaurant for lunch with his colleague, Thomas Braithewaite. Unknown to either of them, Valerie was also there with her friend, Sheila Matheson, from the bank. They didn't see each other, but Sherman caught the unmistakable shrill of Valerie's mean laughter, and immediately paid attention.

The women spoke softly, but he was able to hear. Thomas didn't think it strange – he never did say much over lunch. The men habitually ate in silence.

"He rang my bell, baby," Valerie said.

"Is it serious?" Sheila asked.

"I think it might be. But in any case, it's clear, I've got to leave the accountant."

"When will you tell him? Where will you go?"

"I'll figure it out," Valerie said. "Life's too short for this pretense. I deserve to be happy for real."

And she was right, after all. Everyone deserved to be happy, didn't they?

Too late for Sherman, though. Too late for Elizabeth.

Until that moment in the restaurant, he had never really *hated* another human being.

Unable to finish his lunch, he told Thomas he had a stomach bug and hightailed it back to the office.

That night he sat up planning, "crunching the numbers", working it out in his mind.

First, make sure the insurance was up to date.

Then, investigate easy-to-access drugs that can cause cognitive disorders. Study the dosage required, administer and begin the long-term care process.

Finally, when everyone could see what a caring husband he really was, end this farce, once and for all.

That morning, he and Valerie rose together as usual. She was no longer capable of making breakfast, so he did it, taking care to leave out the usual dose of pharmaceuticals. It wouldn't do to have any trace of unprescribed pills in her digestive tract.

He helped her dress, and convinced her to drive with him to work, saying the bank had called, and they needed her help. He promised to drop her off there.

She was so confused.

After parking at his office – he knew no one would be around at that hour – he swiped in. Instead of entering the building, though, he went back to the car for Valerie.

"Come on, dear," he said. "I'll walk you to the bank."

He wasn't wearing his usual coat. He'd left it in the car. Instead he was wearing an old brown overcoat that had belonged to him when he was a younger man. He also wore a brimmed hat, which he pulled down low to conceal his face.

Sherman walked behind her, speaking to her only when there was no one in hearing range.

"Why do they need my help?" she asked. "I'm not feeling well."

"It's okay, dear, they only need you to balance an account. You'll be home again soon."

Luck was with him as they approached the Don Mills overpass. There was only a small handful of cars on Don Mills, and no other pedestrians yet. The winter sun was habitually late to rise, and in the semidarkness under the streetlights, he knew that even if he was seen, no one would recognize him.

Not wanting to miss the opportunity, he acted as soon as they were on the bridge.

"Sweetheart," he said, grabbing her from behind, "go to Hell."

And now, he thought, savoring the last sip of whiskey, all that remained was to wait out the funeral and cash in the insurance policy.

And hope to hell that dolt Sheila Matheson didn't suspect anything.

***

"What's our next step?" Jerome asked after Robert McQuade and Sheila Matheson had left the Division.

"These are just stories," Mallory said. "Without evidence, they don't mean anything."

"The standard autopsy procedure falls short of giving us what we'd need."

"My money's on cremation. I'm betting he'll wait till the body's released, then make the arrangements quietly."

"Yeah," Jerome said. "He wouldn't rush it – might tip us off."

"Arsenic shows up in the ash after cremation."

"I don't think it's arsenic. At those levels, a blood count high enough to cause flat-out dementia, I doubt whether she'd be able to walk."

"You're right. But if not poison, then what?" Mallory asked.

"Let's call Samden at the Coroner's Office. Put a bug in his ear, ask him to run every test he can think of for any substance known to cause profound dementia and memory loss."

"Good idea," Mallory said. "And be sure to wish him a Happy Freakin' Valentine's Day."

AXE HUSBAND

People often asked Kimberly why she'd left.

Ray was a good man by most accounts.

He seldom drank excessively, opened doors for her, never raised his voice, worked hard to provide.

Besides, they'd been in love. Everyone knew it.

To this day both boys, Phil and Paul, held the divorce against her. They never said so, but she could see it in their eyes. They blamed her for the loss of their father. Gone, for no apparent reason.

Kimberly Johnson never knew what to say, so she held her tongue.

Fifteen years of marriage. You think you know a person. You split your body in half giving him children, hold his hand, listen to his worries, even when you're full to the breaking point with your own. You watch your spending, even though you work hard too, because you know money is one of the things he worries about.

You're gracious to his family and friends, and always careful not to pay too much attention to anyone else, because even though he doesn't mention it, you get the feeling he disapproves.

You walk the dog when it's your turn, feed the cat, clean the house and cook the meals.

None of these things are beyond the call of wifely duty. Billions of women carry out these tasks every day. You seldom complain.

Because you've got a loving husband and decent children.

That makes it all worthwhile.

Kimberly certainly thought she knew Ray. She'd seen him at his worst, when the worries got to be too much and the boss was pressing his buttons and the car broke down.

She'd seen him at his best, full of joy when the boys were born, when they spoke their first words, took their first steps.

She thought she'd seen every side of him.

***

"Get the flashlight, Paul," Phil shouted from the bottom of the stairs.

Phil was the oldest and used to giving orders, which six-year-old Paul cheerfully obeyed.

"I can't find it," Paul said.

"It's in my room. Look on the dresser. It's got new batteries. We'll need it at night."

"Found it!" Paul tore down the stairs, almost falling but catching the handrail just in time.

"I got the fishing rods," Phil said.

"Are we going to see fireflies?" Paul asked.

Phil looked at his father.

"I sure hope so!" Ray said.

Kimberly took the fishing rods from Phil and tucked them into the back of the van.

"This time of year there should be a lot," she said.

Ray nodded. "Yup. Lots."

The boys laughed.

"Come on, guys. Let's get this show on the road."

Ray drove. Kimberly could have used another hour of sleep, but she stayed awake to keep him company. Besides, the boys were so excited – she didn't want to miss the fun.

Choosing a campsite was easy. They'd left the city early enough to beat the crowds, and opted for a large, isolated lot away from traffic, but still within easy walking distance from the bathroom facilities and the beach.

Pitching their new tent was another matter. Ray's family had never camped when he was growing up. Kimberly had plenty of experience, but as every woman knows, it isn't wise to butt in when Dad is instructing the kids, so she offered only subtle hints regarding how best to construct the canvas walls.

After several failed attempts to secure the centre-pole, Ray's normally cheerful mood began to fray.

Being the oldest, Phil was expected to help the most, so he bore the brunt of Ray's jagged comments.

Finally, Kimberly could no longer stay on the sidelines.

"Let me help with that," she said.

Ray snarled something inaudible, but Kimberly stepped in anyway.

Within half an hour, the tent was up and the air mattresses were pumped.

Ray was quiet, but his sulking was preferable to snapping at the boys.

"Can we go to the beach?" Phil said.

"Yeah," Paul chimed in. "Let's go to the beach."

Kimberly looked at Ray. It took some effort on his part, but he finally smiled.

"Come on," he agreed. "Let's change into our swim suits."

Not wanting his mood to slide again, Kimberly herded the boys into the tent to change.

"What about you, Mom?" Phil said.

"It pays to think ahead," she said. "I wore my swim suit under my clothes."

It was a hot day, even in the relative cool of the wooded National park. The kids ran down the beach path, anxious to jump into the water.

"Not too fast, guys," Ray said. "Wait for us."

He was struggling with the beach chairs and a small cooler.

Kimberly had a large beach bag over her shoulder with towels, books and sunscreen. She held out her free hand for the cooler.

"I've got it," he said.

"You're sure?"

"Yeah."

The shady beach path opened onto a stretch of sparkling sand around a silver lake.

"Outstanding," she said. "Great choice!"

She'd never been to this park, but Ray had heard from a friend it was well-maintained and woodsy, with a sandy beach.

Somewhat mollified, he grinned.

Ray set up the chairs and Kimberly smoothed her towel on the sand. It had been a particularly stressful time at work. The competition was heating up and the talk was all about cutting costs.

Which meant more work for everyone, as well as reduced job security.

On top of work stresses, Kimberly also had to spend a fair amount of energy keeping a positive tone at home. Ray had been testy during the past few weeks.

She couldn't blame him, really. He struggled with balancing the family finances, especially as their investments took a beating.

In any event, it was out of character for him to snap at her or the children. She thought it best to bite her tongue and let the difficult period pass.

He needed this vacation as much as she did.

He sat on one of the chairs and pulled the other closer to him.

"Not going to sit?"

"I will later," she said, lying down on the towel. "I'm beat."

"You were tired when we left the house," he said.

Kimberly nodded.

She cracked open her novel, but couldn't focus on the words. The sunshine and the happy sound of children playing smoothed her raw nerves and before long she was dozing happily.

She woke abruptly as Ray nudged her with his right foot.

"Are you watching the kids?" he asked.

His voice was testy again. She didn't know what his problem was, but these mood swings were unpleasant to say the least.

Sighing, she got up and sat in the chair. The seeds of a nasty headache were beginning to take root. Exhaustion. Too many hours of trying to say the right thing, walking on eggshells.

"Hey," Ray said, "if you don't think they need to be supervised, go back to sleep."

"I thought you were watching them," she said.

"I'm tired, too."

"I know you are. Do you want a nap? I'll keep an eye on the boys."

"Forget it." Ray reached into the cooler and pulled out a covered plastic cup.

She knew he'd mixed a drink before-hand. He offered her one, but she shook her head. It would only knock her out.

Ray wasn't much of a drinker normally. She hoped the alcohol would take the edge off his mood.

Kimberly reached for her book.

The boys laughed and played, waving at them from in the water.

"Come on in," Phil said. "It's great!"

She slipped the book into the bag and pulled her t-shirt over her head. The water might energize her.

"Yay! Mom's coming!" Paul shouted.

From the corner of her eye she saw Ray's face contorted in an uncharacteristic scowl. Before she could react, he'd lost the dark look and was smiling.

"Last one in…" he shouted, leaping from the chair.

He had a head start, and besides, Kimberly didn't try very hard to race him. She ran till the water was up to her knees, then walked, letting her skin adjust to the cold.

"Brrr," she said. "Chilly."

"It's fine once you're in," Ray said.

Without warning he turned and knocked her into the water.

"Hey!" she shouted. "Knock it off!"

"Don't be a baby," he said, laughing. "You're not ice cream. You won't melt."

Kimberly didn't know what to say. In their fifteen years of marriage and the two years of dating prior to that, Ray had never handled her with anything but tenderness.

She was offended, but she wasn't hurt. She decided to let the incident pass without an argument.

"Come on, guys," Paul called, waving at his parents.

She waved back and ran to the boys. Ray followed.

***

That evening, Ray paid ten dollars for a large bundle of firewood. Kimberly baked potatoes and barbecued steaks on the Hibachi while Ray sharpened sticks.

After dinner, they roasted marshmallows.

"Who wants to hear a ghost story?" Ray asked.

"I do," Phil said.

Paul shook his head, but seeing his big brother's enthusiasm, he held his tongue. He sat on Kimberly's lap.

"A long time ago…" Ray began.

"How long?" Paul asked.

"Hundreds of years," Ray said.

"Were there TVs?" Paul said.

"Stop interrupting," Kimberly said. She could see Ray was becoming annoyed.

"There were no TVs," Ray said. "No cars, no guns, no video games. People would gather together to tell stories to pass the time. That's how people far from the cities would learn the news. Travelling groups would act out plays, sing songs and tell stories.

"One of those stories has been passed down from father to son for hundreds of years. And now, tonight, it's finally time for me to tell you both the *Story of the Headless Harlot.*"

"What's a harlot?" Paul asked.

"A prostitute," Phil said.

"A lady," Kimberly said.

"A lady," Ray answered, "who isn't a lady. Mwah haha hah…." He held the flashlight under his chin, causing light and shadows to compete for dominance of his features.

"I'm scared," Paul said.

"Shhh!" Phil put his finger to his lips.

"Come on," Kimberly said, lifting Paul from her knee. "I have to use the washroom. I'll take you with me. Maybe we'll see some fireflies."

"It's just a story," Ray said, turning off the flashlight.

"I want to hear it," Phil said.

"Forget it. I wouldn't want to scare anyone."

Great, thought Kimberly. *Now he'll sulk again.*

Still, better that than be up all night because the boys are having nightmares. Paul was only five, too young for stories about decapitating scarlet women.

Sometimes Ray had no sense at all.

When she returned from the bathroom with Paul, she found Ray sitting alone staring at the fire.

"Where's Phil?" she asked.

"Getting ready for bed," Ray said without looking up.

"I'll take him to the bathroom."

"Whatever."

"Paul, you go get into your jammies, too."

The picnic table and campfire were a distance from the tent, on the other side of a minor ridge. Paul was too short to see the tent from where they stood. He pulled his mother's hand, not wanting to cross the distance alone in the darkness.

Kimberly walked him to where the tent stood on higher ground at the edge of the woods.

"You ready for bed?" she called in to Phil.

His answer came as a grunt from inside the tent.

"Come on, then," she said. "I'll walk you to the bathroom while Paul's changing."

"I don't want to be alone," Paul whined.

"Don't worry," she said. "You can change and we'll all go together. You might need to pee again anyway."

Phil emerged from the tent but wouldn't meet Kimberly's eyes.

Her neck tingled.

"What's the matter?" she asked quietly. Voices could carry at night. She didn't want Ray to hear.

"Nothing."

She took Phil's hand in her right one and held out her left for Paul. Together she and the boys covered the distance to the public washrooms. Phil carried the toothbrushes and Paul the washcloths.

When the boys were cleaned up and ready for bed they walked back to the campsite together.

"'Night, Phil," she said, kissing her eldest on the forehead.

"'Night, Mom."

"Have a good sleep, Paul." She pulled the sleeping bag up to his chin and kissed him on the cheek.

"I love you," he said.

Once they were settled, Kimberly considered turning in as well. Ray was in a sour mood and would be lousy company.

Still, if she went to bed without saying goodnight to him he'd really have something to sulk about.

Might as well see if he'd like a cup of tea first.

She zipped up the tent flap and made her way quietly back to Ray. She could see the campfire even over the ridge. The flames had climbed higher since she'd left with the boys.

"Can I make you a cup of tea?" she asked.

Ray didn't look up.

"No thanks," he said.

"Would you like anything before I turn in?"

"Nope."

"OK, then, good night."

"Good night."

During their brief exchange, Ray's eyes did not leave the campfire.

All right then, she thought. *Be like that.*

Kimberly wasn't planning to lose sleep over it.

She woke a few hours later, unsure at first of her surroundings.

The boys were fast asleep, their childish snores barely audible.

Ray hadn't come to bed yet.

"Oh for Pete's sake," she muttered, careful not to wake the boys.

She pulled on her shoes and quietly unzipped the tent flap. She couldn't leave Ray outside all night. He wasn't used to camping. Maybe he'd passed out. It wasn't like him to drink excessively, but she'd lost count of the number of drinks he'd consumed.

Besides, he might set the whole campground on fire.

As she approached the ridge, she could see the flames. They leapt and danced, throwing sparks high into the night-black clearing.

Was Ray asleep near the fire?

Thwack!

Apparently not.

Thwack!

What the hell was he doing?

She peeked over the ridge.

Ray had an axe. He raised it repeatedly, splintering the picnic table.

Thwack!

Kimberly watched in horror. This man was so unlike the husband she thought she knew that she didn't dare to move. His eyes glowed orange in the campfire. His face was a study in rage.

He was saying something. Not muttering, exactly, but not speaking loudly either. His voice was almost a chant. She had to strain to hear.

"Kill the bitch," he said. "Kill the black-hearted whore and her bastard sons. No one will know. Kill her and throw her into the fire where she belongs. Cut off her head and burn it."

Thwack! went the axe.

"Let the whore and her offspring burn in hell."

Thwack!

***

People never understood why Kimberly left Ray the way she did.

It was inexplicable.

She just packed the boys into the mini-van one night during their family holiday and drove away, leaving her husband of fifteen years stranded in the far north, without so much as a good-bye.

No one could figure it out.

No one except for Kimberly.

And maybe Ray.

LOW ROLLER

It isn't just that the holidays bring out the worst in people.

Sure, some of us blame the stress and bustle of the season for causing family arguments, a trail of mini crises that we leave in our wake as we shop, cook and clean.

The painful struggle to maintain permanent smiles throughout a marathon of entertaining.

It isn't easy being gracious for weeks at a stretch.

But we really shouldn't blame it on the holidays. Some people are just miserable all year 'round.

The Christmas season, with its artificial twinkle of good cheer, serves to highlight the fact that some souls are bleak at the best of times.

Staying cheerful is easier for people like me.

I've got no family to speak of, except for Aunt Rachel, and she never puts up much fuss over Christmas. You see, she never married, so her festive table, elaborately decorated as it is, seats only the two of us.

She detests turkey, preferring a nice steak or a bit of ham.

We usually eat in silence, but it's a comfortable silence. I never doubt her love.

It's her sense of tradition that could use a shot in the arm.

***

"Would you like more tea, dear?"

"No thank you, Mattie," I said. I'd be awake half the night as it was, hopped up on caffeine and peeing a blue streak.

"What did you say your name is?" Mattie's daughter, Delilah – forty if she was a day – pointed her pen my way.

"Penelope Canon," I replied, hiding my annoyance for Mattie's sake. Delilah would have been a good-looking woman, except for the permanently pinched look where a smile would have been welcome.

"And how do you know my mother?" she said, scribbling down my name.

I couldn't blame her for being suspicious. From where she sat it would appear odd, me on the young side of thirty-something and claiming a close friendship to Mattie Oaks, a sixty-five-year-old widow of comfortable means and tremendous elegance.

I was tempted to say 'We met in yoga class,' but I chewed on my short-bread cookie instead.

You see, I knew the truth about Delilah.

I knew she seldom, if ever, spent time with Mattie. The only reason she was here today was because of that great unifier – the 'family emergency'.

Delilah's brother, Jordan Oaks, had gone missing.

Again.

"Don't you remember, Delilah?" Mattie answered for me. "I told you about a young woman I met in my pottery class a few years ago."

I glanced around Mattie's stunningly decorated dining room. Casual comfort reminded the visitor she was, after all, a child of the sixties. Her own clay pieces were displayed on every surface, making the space unique. Playful colors blending with earth tones created a sense of warmth.

Just like Mattie.

I, of course, had no potting talent whatsoever. Mucking about, as Mattie called it, wasn't my bag. I'd joined the class for one reason only: to rub elbows with a woman suspected by her employer of stealing pharmaceuticals to smuggle south of the border.

My plan didn't work out. No sooner had I chatted the suspect up than she dropped the class, quit her job and left town.

Meanwhile, my world collided with Mattie's.

She laughed openly at my ridiculous attempts to make clay art. Everything I touched came out looking like an ashtray.

Ironic, since neither Aunt Rachel nor I smoked.

Even after I dropped the class and came clean with Mattie about my reasons for signing up, we remained friends. I think in many ways Mattie is a kindred spirit. Although you'd never guess it to look at the two of us. I'm short and hardly sweet – a rough tough creampuff, as described by an ex-boyfriend – with no taste to speak of and little in the way of artistic talent or grace.

Mattie is tall, slender and the picture of refinement. She takes pride in her keen eye and is able to charm the birds out of the trees.

It would be hard not to like her. She smiles easily, laughs at everything I say and cooks like a master – another skill I'm sorely lacking.

She seldom complains. It was months before I began to get an inkling of her strained relationships with her son and daughter. It was much longer before I knew how bad things really were.

I couldn't figure it out. Mattie was a joy to be around. What the hell was the story with her kids?

Finally I got the picture.

Mattie had married their father when Delilah was fifteen and Jordan only ten. A short time later, Richard was diagnosed with an aggressive form of cancer.

When he died, Delilah blamed Mattie.

Jordan didn't blame anyone. He just shut down.

Maybe he'd always had a bipolar disorder. But it wasn't an obvious problem until after Richard died. From that point on, Jordan's depression presented itself in a variety of behavioral problems. It began with poor marks and a regrettable circle of friends and flowered into drug addiction, alcoholism and gambling.

He'd disappeared twice before.

He was thirty-five. Not bad looking, judging by Mattie's photos, except for the darkness in his eyes.

Jordan hadn't lived with Mattie since he'd dropped out of university. She tried to get help for him, but he'd resisted every effort. They'd argued constantly in those days.

Delilah convinced Mattie that she was enabling Jordan's behavior by continuing to feed and house him.

Mattie asked Jordan to leave.

It was the hardest thing she'd ever done. She'd given her word to her dying husband to care for his children. It was all he'd ever asked of her.

Sometimes life can break your heart.

"Yes," Delilah said, looking up from her notepad. "I remember. You met in pottery class. And you're a private investigator, is that right, Ms. Canon?"

"That's right, Ms. Oak."

I didn't appreciate Delilah's tone. I could put on an attitude, too.

Of course, given my petite stature and casual clothes as compared with her striking height and impeccable dress, my 'tone' might be somewhat less impressive than hers.

"Can you help us find Jordan?" Mattie said.

"Of course. I'll do what I can, Mattie. Just tell me when you last spoke with him, and anything you can about his habits."

Mattie went through the story again.

I sipped my tea and made notes of my own.

Last contact – telephone (Home phone) two days before Christmas. Expected for dinner December 25.

No answer on home or cell phone since.

"What did the police say?"

"They filed the report. They sent out a press release. There has been no response so far."

Mattie poured more tea for Delilah. I put my hand over my cup.

I had everything Mattie was able to give me, and frankly I was tiring of Delilah's company.

"Do you have an extra set of keys for Jordan's apartment?" I asked. "I'd like to start there."

Mattie reached into her purse. She struggled to remove a key from her ring and handed it to me.

"If you don't mind, I'll join you," Delilah said.

"Actually…"

"I've discussed this with Penelope," Mattie said. "I'd prefer if she went alone to Jordan's apartment. That way she can take her time and look for clues. She doesn't need us looking over her shoulder."

"But, Mom…."

"It's been decided, Delilah." Mattie put her teacup down and walked me to the door.

Once out of her step-daughter's sight, she took my hands in hers.

"I don't know what you can do," she said, "but thank you."

***

It had been Mattie's idea to send me alone to Jordan's apartment. Whatever secrets her step-son might have, they were his. They were not to be shared with his judgmental sister. It was one thing for me, a stranger, to rifle through the details of his life. He wouldn't likely take too kindly to Delilah going through his things.

I was grateful. I couldn't imagine doing a thorough job of it with Delilah at my side.

The key turned smoothly in the lock. I opened Jordan's door, taking a moment to study the tidy foyer and main living area.

Most drug addicts I've encountered in the course of my work, and there have been a surprising number, mostly runaways, are not capable of maintaining a decent living space.

At first I was surprised at the cleanliness and order, till I recalled that Mattie, not wanting Jordan to give over to sloth, had hired a regular cleaning lady.

In the novels of yesteryear, when the PI enters a room that is part of his investigation, he'll usually move in a logical pattern. He'll pull on gloves so as not to disturb any evidence and he'll take pains not to miss the slightest clue.

There wasn't going to be anything of interest in this perfectly manicured environment. I locked the door behind me and stepped further into the apartment. Slowly I made my way to the gleaming kitchen, the sparkling bathroom, the polished living room and the perfectly made up bedroom.

Only one room held my interest.

Some things don't change.

Like the appeal of a locked door.

No private investigator can resist it.

Enter me, it seems to command. *Beyond this door are the clues you seek, the answers to your questions.*

I considered leaving Jordan's apartment without breaking into the locked room.

But not seriously.

I found a screwdriver in a tool box in the laundry room. I had the lock off in minutes.

I paused, holding the doorknob for a moment, savoring the sensation of imminent solution.

Then I opened the door.

As I expected, it was a den. A private office, so to speak. The place where Jordan kept everything he really cared about, in one great heaping mess.

Papers. Books. A television. A desk. A computer.

All in no particular order.

It was obvious the cleaning lady wasn't allowed in this room.

I smiled.

It seemed I'd discovered the real Jordan Oaks.

I was grateful for yet another difference between modern investigative work and that done by the gumshoes of the past.

In the last century, the investigator would spend hours sifting through this mess of papers and books, hoping for some scrap of evidence to fall out from the debris.

I headed straight for the desk. The computer was already turned on. I jiggled the mouse to bring the monitor to life.

Jordan's 'inbox' winked at me, strutting on the desktop like a big fat turkey.

I scrolled down past Viagra and anti-depressant ads, looking for anything of a personal nature.

Bingo!

An email from someone by the name of Scott, asking where the hell Jordan was and why he hadn't shown up to watch the game on Tuesday night.

Another, earlier, message from Bill saying he'd be by to collect. With the ominous command to "cough up" the full amount "or else". That one was dated December 23.

And one from someone called Julie, asking Jordan if he was mad about anything. She'd tried calling him, it said, but the voice mail wasn't working.

Voicemail.

Maybe it was full, I thought. I'd have a listen once I was done with the email.

Jordan's PC was connected to a printer on top of a cabinet. I printed all the emails I thought might be relevant, going back to the week before Jordan disappeared.

Then I checked out his deleted folder. Like many people, Jordan stored old emails there once he'd finished with them, rather than removing them permanently.

One in particular was interesting.

Jordan. We're waiting for you. Get your ass down here. Now.

No sender name, but the auto-signature attached was a logo for Zoe's Palace, a downtown strip club and known hangout for dealers.

The message was received on December 24 at 8:25 pm, the night before Jordan went missing.

I printed it. I'd definitely be paying Zoe a visit.

Next, I listened to Jordan's phone messages, taking care not to delete any in case he showed up alive and well and wanting to check his voicemail.

As I'd thought, the voicemail was full. There were three messages offering superb duct cleaning services, two promising to install new windows and doors, one asking for a contribution for the NDP, one from Julie, just asking him to call, and one from Bill.

At least I assumed it was Bill. He didn't leave a name, but he did leave an amount. Fifteen hundred. Cash. To be paid in full.

And he left a time, 7 pm. *I'll be there at 7*, the message said. *Have the $1500 ready in cash. Or else.* The voicemail had tagged the message as "received December 24th".

It was the "or else" that gave Bill away. It was the same wording he'd used in his email. As clichéd as it was, it was still too much coincidence for this girl.

I set the receiver onto its cradle, resting my hand on it as I tried to piece together a likely scenario.

Maybe Jordan didn't have the $1500. Maybe he'd gone to ground to avoid meeting with Bill. Not that Bill wasn't a nice guy. His voice sounded nice. Well, not so much 'nice' as 'scary'.

Yes. Definitely scary.

Had Jordan decided to take a Christmas vacation rather than spending Christmas Eve with an obvious mob-muscle man?

Or had he dropped in at Zoe's Palace to meet 'the gang' for a drink? Maybe he was still there.

I glanced around the room, taking in the stacks of paper on every surface.

It would be a shame not to spend at least a little time going through them, since I was here anyway.

I reached for a page. A look at it told me Jordan was paying his phone bill. So he presumably had an income.

The next item was his internet invoice, likewise paid up to date.

As were his credit card, his on-line gambling tab and his cable TV.

This was one highly-functioning drug addict.

So why duck out on Bill?

Surely he could have put off paying his credit card for a month. That payment alone would have covered what the mob-man was asking for.

It didn't make any sense.

I looked again at the stack of paid invoices. All had been paid well in advance of the due date.

There was only one reasonable explanation.

Mattie must be paying his bills.

I'd bet my skinny jeans on it.

I pulled my smartphone out of my pocket and dialed her number.

Her voice sounded strange on the phone, like she didn't want to speak freely.

"Is Delilah still there?" I asked.

"Yes. We're about to have dinner."

"Can she hear me?"

"No."

"Ok. In that case, I'll ask you a question, and you just say 'yes' or 'no'. Mattie, were you paying Jordan's bills?"

"Yes."

"Does Delilah know that?"

"No."

"Were there any gambling debts?"

"Yes."

"Big ones?"

"No. I have to go now. We're having dinner."

Mattie put the phone down and I heard the click. Then, almost imperceptibly, I heard the second click.

Damn! Delilah had been listening on an extension.

I opened a 'notes' file on my smartphone. Using the tiny keyboard, I tried to map out a plan. It seemed highly unlikely that we'd find Jordan, as least until he wanted to be found. But I'd made a promise to Mattie, and I intended to keep it.

My notes were rough, but I knew what they meant.

First, I'd have to pay a visit to Zoe's, if only to find out whether Jordan ever did show up there.

I'd have to get in touch with Julie, by replying to her email, and ask to meet with her. She might have some insight into Jordan's circle of friends.

I'd email Bill while I was at it. Just a cryptic note, from Jordan, to see what reaction I got.

I needed to have a straight talk with Mattie. She said the gambling debts were not large, but of course she hadn't been free to elaborate. I had a sneaking feeling between the drugs, gambling and whatever else Jordan had been up to that Mattie was footing a pretty significant bill.

It probably wasn't hurting her. My sense was that she had a solid financial buffer.

Just the same, Mattie had a good reason not to want Delilah to know she'd been supporting Jordan.

Big Sister was not going to like it.

Hmmmmm....

I wondered.

Was that the first time Delilah had listened in on Mattie's conversations?

My Aunt Rachel has a saying: *A goose will honk and a duck will quack.*

And Delilah was a sneak. She'd already proven that.

Maybe she knew about Mattie paying Jordan's bills.

How would she feel about seeing her inheritance being syphoned off by a drug addicted gambler who couldn't keep himself in toilet paper?

My guess was she'd be ticked.

All those years of waiting for Daddy's money to come through, patiently watching Step-Mom live the good life of fine clothes and pottery classes and luxury living. Knowing there was plenty to come, in time.

Only to see her baby brother squander the lion's share.

Would anything be left for Delilah? Or would she get the short end of the stick again?

Yes.

I'd definitely pay a visit to Zoe's Palace.

But first....

My bike was parked in the visitors' lot. I started the ignition and donned my helmet, heading back in the direction I'd come from.

When I arrived at Mattie's, Delilah had already left.

Mattie didn't come to the door when I rang the bell. I dug in my pocket for my keychain, quickly locating the extra key Mattie had given me "in case she locked herself out".

Delilah wouldn't have known I had it.

How could Delilah know that, if anything happened to Mattie, it was me, rather than her step-children, she placed her trust in?

I found Mattie on the kitchen floor. She'd splashed tea on the tabletop when she fell. She was still breathing.

Beside the teacup was a single white sheet of paper, with one sentence scrawled in Mattie's usually graceful handwriting:

I'm sorry, Jordan.

I dialed 9-1-1.

The paramedics were able to revive Mattie and induce vomiting. It took a while, but at the hospital they got her stomach pumped and were able to save her life.

She told the police how Delilah must have slipped something into her tea.

I guess Delilah thought it would go down as suicide.

After all, Mattie was grieving over the loss of her troubled step-son. She was experiencing guilt over her failure to keep Jordan on the straight and narrow.

We later learned that Jordan had visited his sister on Christmas Eve. She must have thought it strange that he could afford to bring her an expensive gift, given that he didn't have a job.

But, of course, she knew where the money came from.

She'd killed Jordan that night and somehow dragged his body to her car. He was slight, thanks to years of substance abuse and poor eating habits. She'd driven to the countryside and found an isolated spot to drop him off. He wouldn't be found till spring, if then.

At least Mattie's money would be safe from his abuse.

And, with Mattie out of the way, Delilah would finally have her inheritance.

It might have worked. She might have gotten away with it.

Luckily for Mattie, though, she has a friend in low places.

PREPARED

"Helen," she said, "I've come to prepare you."

The woman spoke in an urgent voice. Her hair was a mixture of silver and gold, advancing years in denial, given the lie by timeless blue eyes.

Helen had never seen her before, but she seemed familiar.

Helen woke with a start and squinted at the bedside clock. 2 am. No sounds, other than the natural creaking of an aging house — old, but with good bones.

Then she remembered. Zee had called at 11 to say she would be staying overnight with her friend Claire. Helen guessed her daughter was likely spending the night with her boyfriend, Sam, but Zee was a young woman. She could do as she pleased.

Helen was grateful that, at the age of 20, her daughter still called when she wasn't coming home. Zee never gave her cause to worry.

She'd raised Zee to be an independent woman. Her daughter was strong, beautiful and thoughtful.

Helen reached for her crutches and strapped them on. She was careful to use both when she was home alone. How embarrassing would that be, to fall down in the bathroom with her drawers around her ankles?

She did her business and washed her hands, ruminating on the face from her dream. So familiar, and yet she couldn't place it. A depth of kindness in those eyes.

She shook her head, unable to match the face to memory. She glanced in the mirror at her own blue-grey eyes and golden hair. Well, chemical gold, but still vibrant, thanks to Zee. Zee would not allow Helen to let herself go.

Leaning on her left crutch, she reached for a brush and smoothed the tangles before heading back to bed.

The physical struggle of moving on crutches stirred her heart in an uncomfortable palpitation. The moment passed. Soon she was asleep.

"Helen, please listen to me." The woman touched her shoulder.

"What do you want?"

"Your Father sent me to prepare you."

A quiet rage took hold of Helen, tightening her fists. She stood tall, as she often did in her dreams, without crutches, without pain. A force to be reckoned with.

"Don't mention my father," she said. "He was a wife-beater, a child molester and a drunken bastard. I don't have time to remember him."

"Your heavenly Father is sorry for your suffering, Helen. He knows pain has been a part of your life."

"How can He call himself a loving God? My entire life has been about misery. From those early years of abuse, to this illness that makes me a burden. A burden to the husband who left me, and now to his child."

"You're not a burden, Helen. You are loved. And your life," the woman added, "has not been all about pain."

"That's true," Helen nodded, her anger subsiding. "I have Zee. I am thankful for that."

"Helen," the woman said, "I need to prepare you..."

"It's all right," Helen said. "I've been prepared for years. Since this illness claimed me. Tell Our Father He can take me when He's ready."

"But Zee...."

"Zee will be all right," Helen said, suddenly calm. "She knew this would happen. I've always been honest with her, taught her to be strong."

Helen smiled at the thought of her daughter. Zee was doing well at University. Helen had prepared her for this day. She never wanted to be a burden to Zee. It was time to let her girl have a life of her own.

Throughout the years of bitterness and sorrow, there had always been one gift. Zee. Helen's pride and joy, her offering to the world.

Knowing she would leave behind such a fine young woman made it easier for Helen to face mortality.

"I've become tired of this struggle," she said. "Tell Our Father, if He can forgive me for being a stubborn, angry fool, then I can forgive Him for giving me this pain. I'm ready to make my peace."

"Helen," the angel said, for she must be an angel, so lovely, with such kindness in her sad eyes. She looked like someone Helen knew. "Please hear me. You need to be prepared."

"It's ok," Helen said, letting the dream-angel drift away. "Whenever you're ready, take me to Him. I'm prepared."

With a feeling of contentment, Helen took her leave of the angel, allowing her mind to wander into other rooms, other dreams....

***

"I'd like to leave now," Zee said, glancing over her shoulder at a young man on the other side of the room.

"Are you ok?" Sam asked. "You seem preoccupied."

"I'm all right. Just tired. It's late. I've got classes tomorrow."

"Did you call your Mom?"

"I told her I was staying with Claire."

"Good. It's noisy in here. I'll go outside and call a cab."

Sam kissed Zee on the forehead. She was one in a million, beautiful, kind, studious and loving. He was a lucky guy.

She watched him leave the party, hoping he wouldn't be gone too long.

"Hi, Zee."

She nearly groaned out loud as the other man approached, but good manners kicked in and she managed to restrain herself.

"Hi, Richard," she said.

"Who's the guy?"

"That's my boyfriend, Sam."

"Some boyfriend. No offense, but he looks like a girl. Why'd he ditch you?"

"He's calling a cab. We're leaving. Now you'll have to excuse me."

Zee stood. She could feel her Scots-Irish blood rising. Her mother hadn't raised her to tolerate this kind of nonsense. Richard had been a nuisance for weeks, but now he was becoming insufferable. She didn't want to make a scene, but she would if she had to.

"Take it easy, Zee," he said. "I just want to talk. You've been avoiding me."

"Stop following me, Richard. I saw you at the library today."

"I was studying," he said. "It's a free country."

"Excuse me," she said, trying to push past him.

Richard held her arm. "You never gave me a chance," he said.

"Let go of me."

The knife's blade was sharp and mercifully swift. She hardly felt it slide past her rib-cage and into her heart. Her hearing became muted and at the same time strangely acute.

She was aware of horrified shouts as her friends looked up in alarm.

Her blood crashed in her ears, drowning out their cries. Her closest friend Claire rushed to her side. She watched as someone ran to get Sam. He pushed through the crowd and knelt, in time to hear her whisper.

"My mother...."

APPEARANCES

"No, that's all right, Val," Janie said. "Life does, after all, go on. I'm glad you and Carmen thought of me, being in the neighborhood and all. Stop by and we'll have coffee."

Janie put the phone down and glanced around the living room. It was still tidy from the other day.

The kitchen was clean but disheveled. She ran hot water and washed the dishes, starting up the coffee maker. Replacing the lid on a small bottle, she put it away in the cupboard.

***

"How did she sound?" Carmen said.

"Quite chipper, actually. It's as if nothing happened. Did you see her the other day, chatting with that handsome Minister and his wife? Talk about keeping a stiff upper lip."

"Everyone copes with these things differently. I don't envy Janie, all alone in that big house. Shepp was her world."

"Hmm…"

"You disagree?"

"Well," Val said, "it's not like they were together all that long. She snapped him up like shoes on sale."

"You think she married him for his money?"

"He sure as hell had enough of it. And she was dirt-poor, working her ass off to make ends meet at that hole-in-the-wall bookstore."

"Her luck turned around, didn't it?" Carmen said. "Right after they married, she managed to line up an agent and a publisher. Then winning that big literary award…"

"Did you see Shepp's kids, Lacey and Ron, at the funeral? How old are they?"

"They're both still in University, so they must be in their early twenties."

"They barely spoke two words to Janie the entire time. Having such a young step-mother probably doesn't sit well with them. I wonder whether she'll inherit everything."

"I'm sure Shepp provided for his children. After all, they're still in school."

"I'm just saying – the bulk of the estate will go to her. And from where I stand, she's not entirely lost in grief." Val pulled into a quiet neighborhood and parked on the street. "Here we are."

"What a lovely house!" Carmen said, studying the expanse of landscaping that led to the sprawling, white stuccoed building.

***

Through the living room window, Janie watched the women approach. She pulled her shoulders up, reminding herself to show a friendly smile. She'd never been fond of Val. On the other hand, Carmen was nice enough.

"Come in," Janie said. "Such a nice day. I was working in the garden this morning. What brings you ladies to my neck of the woods?"

"Actually, Janie," Val said, "we came to ask you a favor."

"And you came all this way? I'm glad. It gives us a chance to visit. How do you like your coffee?"

"That smells wonderful, Janie," Carmen said. "Cream and sugar, please."

"Black for me," Val said.

The three women sat in a breakfast nook off Janie's marble-finished kitchen.

"I've never seen your place," Carmen said. "It's really nice."

"Thank you. Shepp built it for Angie, of course. Everything was to her taste, but I have to admit, I'm fond of it. She had a decorator's touch."

"You've probably added your own style over the years."

"Not really. A blanket here, a picture there – that's about it. Kind of strange, really, settling into another woman's surroundings. But my focus has always been my writing, so it's worked out well in that way."

"Actually," Val said, "that's why we're here. The annual CanLit Conference is coming up. We need a guest of honor and we're hoping you'll agree…"

"Me? I'm stunned. I don't know what to say. Thank you. But that's in July, isn't it?"

"Yes. We wanted to ask you sooner, but with Shepp so sick – we'll understand if it's too short notice."

"No, it isn't that. It's just that it's so soon after… I don't know…"

"We have a couple of other names we can try," Carmen said. "We were really hoping for you, though."

"I'm deeply honored. That's still two months away – plenty of time for this old hack to pull herself together. I'll do it. You must have been worried, not having the spot filled on the program."

"Frankly, we spoke to Mel Hanson a while ago. He was ready to step up if we couldn't get you. We'll ask him to MC the event instead."

"This is entirely unexpected and so kind of you. I'll be honored to accept."

"It's settled, then," Carmen said. "We'll add you to the program right away. Can we trouble you to throw together a bio, about a hundred words?"

"Of course. I'll email it to you tonight."

"And we'll need five hundred words on *Thieves In The Afternoon*," Val said. "You know, the creative process, the idea, that sort of thing."

Janie stared into her coffee mug. That book had taken eight long years to write, edit and revise. Dark years of sick obsession, lost in the literary dance of pathos and Eros, good and evil, the seemingly endless struggle to create something real.

Hungry years of scrimping, barely able to pay the rent on her meagre salary from the bookstore, pouring every waking moment into an effort with no reason to expect a payoff. Few friends, no social life, no love...

Then two more years given over to the hopeless attempt to break into a market that was too small, too closed to allow for entry by an 'unknown'.

In the end, it was only Shepp's connections that brought her work to light. He helped find a publisher. His name gave her exposure. For this she would always be grateful.

"That'll take a bit longer," she said. "How soon do you need it?"

"Can you do it by Wednesday?"

"I can send it tomorrow, if you like."

"Perfect," Carmen said. "Now we can talk about other things. How are you holding up?"

"I'm ok," Janie said. "The service went well. Shepp would have been proud. The kids headed back to residence right afterwards. Their semester is wrapping up. They have exams."

"They seem like nice kids," Val said.

"Yes," Janie agreed. "Shepp and Angie did a good job with them."

"You did a good job, too," Carmen said. "I hope they appreciate you."

"I often think I could have done more. But they were already in their teens when I came into the picture. They have their own ideas. We're not as close as I'd like."

"I'm sure they'll come around," Carmen said. "It's this entire generation. They aren't maturing as early as we did. Eventually they'll realize how much you've done for them."

"I believe they will. It's just that they're so busy now, with exams and all."

"Well," Val said, "I have a meeting this afternoon. Thank you for the coffee, Janie. And thank you for saving our bacon on the conference. We were counting on you."

"That's right," Carmen said. "We've been keeping our fingers crossed. I'm glad it all worked out. If there's anything we can do to make it easier for you, just let us know."

"Don't worry," Janie said. "This is the shot in the arm I needed after everything with Shepp. There is no better validation of one's work than being honored by one's peers."

***

Val unlocked the car doors and tossed her purse into the back seat. The two women were quiet as they pulled away from the house.

When they turned onto the main street, Carmen broke the silence.

"I hate to say it," she said, "but that was strange."

"I told you so," Val said. "Even the kids couldn't wait to get away from her. Not a flicker of emotion – very cold."

"Maybe it hasn't hit her yet," Carmen said. "Maybe she hasn't faced it that he's really gone."

"Maybe, but she didn't think twice about the 'guest of honor' slot. Anything to further the career and image."

"Do you regret asking her?"

"Not at all," Val said. "I'm as mercenary as the next gal. We need a big name and Janie's about as big as it gets.

Shepp's death adds to the mystique, if you know what I mean."

"Mm-hmm," Carmen nodded. She wasn't comfortable with Val's harsh judgement of Janie, but she had to admit, there was something odd about the woman. Like everyone, Carmen had her own ideas about grief. Janie just didn't fit the bill.

***

Janie watched the women drive away. She sighed. Her smile fell away like the lace of the curtain, leaving her face dark and drawn.

They were good women, she thought. So kind. And such an honor. They must have been nervous, holding the position of guest of honor open so long. How could she refuse, under the circumstances?

Thieves In The Afternoon was a runaway success, riding the *New York Times* bestseller list for months during the previous year. Excellent marketing by the publisher Shepp had lined up for her, coupled with relentless interviews and appearances on her part had lifted it above the rest.

Shepp would not allow her to give up. Throughout his long illness, he kept reminding her she deserved success.

What did any of it mean without Shepp? Ahead of her stretched only loneliness, more decades of writing in a void. Her heart was empty, drained from all those years of pouring its contents onto the page, rinsed clean by grief that no one else would see.

Even Shepp's children had deserted her. They'd never accepted her, but if Shepp had lived long enough, eventually they would have come around. Now it was too late.

Janie reached into the kitchen cupboard and removed a handful of tiny bottles she'd been accumulating for the past few months. She lined them up on the counter, touching the lids lovingly.

She paused for a moment, still unsure. That very morning she'd planned to swallow them all and end this misery. Now, though, Val and Carmen had come into her kitchen bearing a gift – the gift of kindness. The gift of respect for her efforts.

The gift of friendship.

Maybe these things were enough to live for. Maybe friendship could carry her past this sense of hopelessness.

She would invite the children to the ceremony. That might open the door to bring them closer.

Carefully she removed the lids from each of the bottles. She poured the contents into a bowl and carried them to the bathroom. She didn't dare leave them in the cupboard, where they might present temptation on another day.

Janie dumped the pills and flushed them away.

She had work to do.

WATERMELON WEEKEND

Arthur Ellis Award Finalist for Best Short Story, 2014

My mother believed in the irrepressible power of love.

Some might have called her a romantic, but that wasn't the case. When it came to distinguishing between love and romance, she could not have cited the definitions. She wasn't able to manipulate semantics in that way.

But she knew the meaning of the word.

I was the eldest of four boys raised by Elizabeth "Bessie" Fender.

I appeared on the scene when she was nineteen. At four months pregnant, she married my father, John Fender, for whom I was named. Dad finished high school and enlisted in the Armed Forces to provide for us.

Eighteen months later he was dead. The only mementos I have are a pair of pictures on my nightstand. There's one of him with my mother, laughing on my grandfather's porch, and another where he's in full uniform about to ship out to Cyprus.

Oh, and the story of how he died – that's mine as well, though I usually keep it to myself. There's nothing noble in the concept of friendly fire. When his Canadian peace-keeping unit was hit that day, he wasn't the only casualty. A couple of civvies went down, but they aren't listed by name in the letter Mom received.

That's another story, and not one I like to dwell on. I never knew Dad, but I have to give him credit. According to my mother, he was handsome and brave, and, like her, he believed in love.

Because I had no father, Grandpa did his best to step into the role. He taught me to fish and how to fix things. He wasn't a violent man. I don't believe I ever saw him angry, not really. Still, he took the time to talk to me about self-defense, in the way I imagined my own father would have if he'd lived.

"I don't go for weapons," he said. "If your enemy is bigger and stronger than you are, he's going to take your knife and use it against you.

"If you must fight with a weapon, don't let go of it no matter what. Consider it an extension of your hand. And don't hesitate to use it."

I nodded as if I understood.

"And Johnny," he added, "never forget: It's always best to walk away from a fight. A real man doesn't have to prove himself."

In my childish mind, I knew he was wrong. A man did have to prove himself.

"If you find yourself in a situation where you have to fight, for God's sake, fight hard. If you knock a man down, make sure he stays down."

"Have you ever been in a fight, Grandpa?" I asked.

"Once or twice, son."

He smiled, pointing at the kitchen cupboard. "Go get me the Phillips screwdriver," he said. "That hinge is loose. I know your mother. She'll be nagging us if she sees it."

It was Friday morning more than twenty years ago, when I was twelve going on thirteen. I could hear my eight-year-old brother, Nicky, crashing around in the bathroom. He was supposed to be brushing his teeth, but it sounded more like he was dismantling the plumbing.

The twins, David and Dale, were five. They were good boys, self-sufficient, although they liked to follow Nicky around at times, to his annoyance.

David was the quiet one, content to be in a room with his family. Dale was more talkative, interested in what was going on around him.

Nicky, for the most part, was a sullen child. He didn't cause trouble, but I guess you could say he had a chip on his shoulder. He liked to be left alone. The only person he really related to was our mother.

That Friday morning more than twenty years ago, we were packing for a weekend at the cottage. Grandpa owned a place up in Muskoka. Mom had a key and a standing invitation to take us there any time she liked.

We spent many weekends at Grandpa's cottage. In the old days he used to come with us, doing all the things a father would do. He taught us to play baseball, hauling out his pride and joy: a collectable 1938 *Louisville Slugger* his father had bought him when he first joined Little League.

He used to kid us, saying we had to be "this tall" before he'd let us hold the bat.

He always relented, to our delight. That's what Grandpas are for.

By the time I was twelve, Grandpa wasn't well anymore, and he didn't come up too often. He still liked to know we were using the place, though.

Mom had recently started dating Phil, a thirty-something salesman who was employed by a drug manufacturing company. No one at the pharmacy where she worked knew they were seeing each other. She'd told us about Phil earlier that week, but warned us not to say a word to Grandpa, at least until she was sure it would work out.

Even though Mom was a knockout at thirty-one, a single mother of four boys doesn't get many romantic offers, so she was excited to be dating again.

It was to be our first weekend together with Phil. He seemed like a nice enough guy. I could tell Mom was hoping it would get serious.

"Remember," she confided, "let's not put any pressure on the relationship. It's our secret for now. Don't mention it to Grandpa, or anyone."

I nodded.

I was glad to see Mom happy.

Not so my brother, Nicky. He'd been in a foul mood all week.

"Come on," I said, tapping on the bathroom door. "I need in there. The twins are already in the van."

Nicky didn't answer. A moment later the door opened and he came out, deliberately bumping into me.

I tended to make allowances for my half-brother. According to Grandpa, who seldom had a hard word for anyone, Nicky's father was a "no-good womanizing bum gambler". Steve did time for petty theft and car-jacking. His brief marriage to my mother had ended badly.

A few years later she met Brayden, a handsome musician. He was a nice fellow who paid attention to me and Nicky, which most guys wouldn't do.

When the ultra-sound revealed Mom was carrying his twins, Brayden screwed off. We have no idea where he went. We haven't seen him since.

I think the twins have it worse than Nicky does. At least Nicky's father didn't disappear. It must really suck to be so low on the totem pole.

Mom said the responsibility was too much for Brayden.

I have my own opinion. There are men who face their duties – men like my father and Grandpa – and there are those who don't. It's as simple as that.

I seldom think of Brayden. When I do, I admit it's with a certain measure of disdain.

"Get your stuff," I said. "Tell Mom I'll be right there."

Nicky grabbed his bag and stomped down the stairs.

So that's how we ended up in Mom's minivan on a sunny Friday morning in July. Two adults, four boys and one big hairy dog – our golden retriever, Fanny.

Nicky's mood lifted once we were on our way. He and I played *Mario* on our Gameboys. Dale fell asleep and David worked on a word search.

"Where do you want to shop?" Phil asked.

We were in Barrie with still a long way to go.

"There's a Sobeys up ahead," Mom said. "Do you boys want anything in particular?"

"Watermelon," Nicky said, smiling at the thought.

"Yes, watermelon," I agreed.

"Watermelon it is!" Phil said.

David clapped his hands.

Phil grinned at us in the rear view mirror. I wasn't sure why Mom had let him drive. After all it was our car, and Mom was a good driver.

But he seemed to know his way around, at least so far.

"Do you boys want to come in?" Mom said.

"No, we'll be all right here," I said.

"OK. Keep an eye on your brothers. If the car gets too hot, open a door."

"I'll stay with the boys," Phil said.

As soon as Mom went into the store, Phil pushed his seat back and closed his eyes. It could be a tedious drive if you weren't used to it.

171

Mom was in the store about a half an hour. When she returned, Nicky let out a low whistle.

"Holy crap!" I said.

Mom had gone all out. The buggy was piled high with food.

Nicky and I helped load the groceries into the van.

At the bottom of the buggy were three big green watermelons.

I should mention, Grandpa's cottage has a dock where he kept his boat tied up. The water there is deep and not too full of reeds.

That's where we learned to swim, doing cannon-ball jumps into the cold lake on a hot day.

Some of my best memories involve munching on watermelon with my legs dangling over the edge of that dock.

So yes, we were happy to see the watermelon.

I caught Nicky's eye. He was smiling for a change.

David fell asleep north of Barrie. I lost interest in playing with the Gameboys. I'd recently been teaching myself to play chess, so I challenged Nicky to a duel.

He was a better sport than I was, losing without complaint.

Before we knew it, we could see Go Home Lake. Within twenty minutes we'd be at the cottage.

What could be more thrilling for a boy than arriving at a crystalline lake with hours of sunlight still ahead and nothing to do but run, swim and play?

We hurried to change into our trunks and headed for the dock.

"Keep an eye on your brothers," Mom said.

"I will."

"Dale has trouble climbing out of the water."

"I know."

"I'll bring down some watermelon in half an hour."

"Hooray!" the twins shouted.

That evening Mom surprised us with a rare treat – six huge steaks on the barbecue. We ate till our stomachs were distended: baked potatoes, sour cream and corn on the cob.

"Anyone want more watermelon?" Phil asked.

Without waiting for an answer, he went to fetch a large bowl from the fridge.

Nicky and I groaned at the sight of the juicy red melon. Still, we couldn't help ourselves.

"You boys will be awake peeing all night long," Mom laughed, reaching for a piece.

"Let's hope not." Phil winked at Mom.

She giggled.

I bit into another piece of melon.

Nicky and I washed the dishes while Mom and Phil set up the DVD player.

It wasn't easy finding movies we all liked. Nicky and I would watch just about anything, but the twins got frightened easily. Especially Dale.

Mom finally decided on *Mrs. Doubtfire*.

"Be careful with that knife," Mom said.

I glanced at Nicky, who was carrying the big carving knife toward the sink. It was slick with watermelon juice.

Worried he might hurt himself, I reached for it.

He turned the handle toward me and I dipped the knife into the soapy water, careful not to cut myself.

We have a rule in our house: only Mom and I are allowed to handle the sharp knives. Rather than drying it, Nicky left it standing in the rack.

"Who wants popcorn?" Mom asked.

"We do!" my brothers shouted.

It isn't easy keeping boys fed. Grandpa used to accuse us of having hollow legs.

"Where'd you put your dinner?" he would joke, watching us go back to the stove for seconds.

The movie was a lot of laughs. Even Nicky enjoyed it. By comparison with Steve and Brayden, Robin Williams as Mrs. Doubtfire looked like some kind of Super-Dad.

The northern air was weighing on us, so after the movie Mom ordered us to brush our teeth and get to bed. Nicky and I shared a room near the kitchen, closest to the bathroom. Fanny usually slept on the floor between our single beds. David and Dale had bunk beds in the middle room. The third small room off the living room, farthest from the kitchen, was Grandpa's.

Mom had the master bedroom off the other side of the living room. The cottage had been designed by Grandpa back when Grandma was alive. The big room had belonged to them in those days, but Grandpa seldom came up anymore. When he did, he was happy to use the little room.

Being the oldest, I sometimes stayed up late watching movies with Mom, but it was obvious she wanted private time with Phil, so I didn't argue. Besides I was tired, and Nicky's mood was getting dicey.

I lay awake, listening to adult chatter in the other room. The sound was alien to me, but not unpleasant. Mom and Phil kept the TV volume low. Nicky was asleep in no time and I followed not long after, seduced by the honest fatigue of a day spent in the sunshine.

I don't know what woke me. Maybe it was some minor twitch of Nicky's or maybe Fanny rolled over on the floor. Our dog wasn't much of a talker. When she needed attention, she would give me a look. I don't think I ever heard her whine, and I could count the times she'd barked on one hand.

For whatever reason, I found myself suddenly awake, long after everyone else had gone to sleep.

Nicky had a tendency to get cranky if he didn't get his ten hours, so I crept silently out of bed to the kitchen to check the time.

The clock on the stove said 2:15 am.

I turned toward the bathroom and, as I did, I heard a whisper coming from the twins' room.

I thought I must be imagining it – there was no way either David or Dale would be awake at that hour. I was about to dismiss it when there it was again, the unmistakable sound of a whisper coming from the middle bedroom.

David normally slept on the top bunk, being the braver of the two, and Dale was on the bottom.

Not sure of what I'd heard, and not wanting to wake them, I tiptoed to the doorway and peeked inside.

The twins had a nightlight, a plastic cartoon image, plugged into the outlet near the baseboard. By its light, and to my shock, I saw Phil stretched out on the bottom bunk beside my little brother.

I couldn't see his hands.

Dale saw me before Phil did. My brother's eyes were frightened, and there were tears glistening in the faint light.

Innocent me – I had no idea what was going on. But it didn't look right.

"Dale, are you sick?" I asked.

Phil stood, knocking his head on the top bunk and waking David.

"Dale was crying," he answered, too quickly. "I came to check on him."

"I'll get Mom."

"No need. Everything's all right now."

Dale still hadn't said a word.

"Was it your stomach?" I asked. Dale was sometimes prone to gas, which made him whiney.

He shook his head.

"What was it?" I insisted.

"I want to sleep with you and Nicky," he said.

"Me too," David chimed in.

Something wasn't right. I glanced at Phil and was not reassured by what I saw in his eyes. He was wearing a guilty look, the kind Nicky wore when we caught him red-handed eating the last of the cookies.

"I'll get Mom," I repeated.

Phil grabbed my shoulder as I turned.

"I said there's no need to wake your mother. Everything's all right now."

I have a real thing about being touched by strangers. The only man I'd ever admired and felt loved by was my Grandpa, and he wasn't the touchy-feely sort. He was far more likely to hand me a tool and let me work beside him. That was how we expressed our affection.

I shook Phil's hand off, probably with more force than I intended.

"Hey there," he said. "Just wait a minute."

"Leave me alone."

"What's going on?" I heard my mother's sleepy voice calling from the master bedroom. "Is everyone all right? I knew someone would have trouble sleeping after all that watermelon." She approached the twins' bedroom, pulling her robe over her shoulders.

"Everything's all right," Phil said. "I got up to use the bathroom and heard Dale crying. I came to check on him."

"I want my Mommy," Dale said, becoming hysterical at the sound of our mother's voice.

"There, there, baby. It's all right. Mommy's here now."

"Stay with me, Mommy."

"Stay with me," David repeated Dale's request, minus the tears.

"Is your tummy OK?"

Dale nodded.

"Do you need to use the bathroom?"

He shook his head.

"Do you have a headache?"

Again, the head shake.

"I think you've had a nightmare, sweetheart," she said, hugging my brother. "You close your eyes now and get back to sleep."

"It wasn't a nightmare, Mommy. It was Phil. He scared me."

My stomach tightened.

By now, Nicky was awake as well. He turned on the light and stood in the kitchen near the counter, a wary look on his face. Fanny was at his side.

"Phil was checking on you, dear," Mom said to Dale. "There's nothing to be afraid of."

"He hurt me. I want to sleep with John and Nicky."

Mom let go of Dale and stood, her full height falling short of Phil's by nearly a foot.

"What do you mean, Dale? How did Phil hurt you?"

"He wouldn't leave me alone." Dale began to wail uncontrollably. It was obvious we weren't going to get anything coherent out of him.

"What did you do?" Mom said to Phil, her voice cold in a way I'd never heard before.

"Oh, for Christ's sake, Bessie, the boy had a bad dream. I was checking on him. You baby them all too much."

"Mom," I said, reluctant to interfere, but unable to remain silent, "I saw Phil. He was under the covers with Dale. Dale was crying."

"What do you mean, under the covers?"

I looked at my feet. My vocabulary would not allow me to elaborate.

"Go." My mother pointed at the doorway, her eyes fastened on Phil's face. "Get your clothes on and get out."

"Where can I go?" Phil said. "We only brought your car."

"You can sleep in the van for tonight. In the morning, we'll call you a cab, and you can catch a bus in town."

"This is ridiculous!" he shouted. "I didn't do anything wrong."

"I don't know whether you did or didn't," Mom said, "but I want you out of my house. Do I need to call the police?"

I edged closer to the phone.

"Police?" Phil said, stepping towards our mother. "Are you threatening me?"

Fanny barked – only once. It was such an unusual sound I couldn't help but jump.

Nicky's shoulders stiffened. He slid closer to the dish rack. He caught my eye, and I knew what he was thinking.

Silently, I shook my head. I remembered my grandfather saying a weapon is only as good as the person holding it. If your enemy is bigger and stronger, he will likely take it and use it against you.

It was always better, according to Grandpa, to simply run, and if you couldn't run, then use your brain.

"Let's all settle down," I said in what I hoped was a smooth voice. "Come on, Dale. You've had a bad dream. You and David can sleep with me and Nicky tonight."

In my mind's eye, I saw the privacy latch my grandfather had attached to our bedroom door. "A boy your age needs to be able to lock the door every now and again," he said. I figured once the boys were in our room, we could lock it. If necessary, we could use my cell phone to call the cops.

Phil had other plans.

"Settle down?" he mimicked. "Who the hell do you think you're talking to?" Phil pushed Mom out of the bedroom. She hit her head on the door frame and fell onto the living room floor.

Fanny leapt forward, placing her body between Phil and our mother. Her efforts won her a kick in the ribs. She yelped, but did not move.

"That's enough," I said.

Nicky took another step toward the kitchen counter.

David scrambled down from the top bunk and ran to our mother.

"You little shit," Phil snarled in my direction, his congenial mask now long gone. "I could kill the lot of you and no one would even know I was here."

Dale let out a fresh howl.

"You hear me? I could start with Dale here, snap him in half with one hand and keep on going till I put every one of you miserable bastards down."

Phil reached for Dale, pulling him from the bottom bunk. He dug his fingers into Dale's fragile shoulder and pulled him past our mother into the living room.

"What's with this brat?" he said. "Doesn't he ever stop whining?"

He lifted Dale into the air and shook him, yelling, "Shut the fuck up."

Dale held his breath, doing his best not to cry.

Mom stood up.

"Please, Phil," she said, in her most reasonable Mom voice, "let's get some sleep. We're wound up. It's probably the watermelon."

"You stupid cow," Phil sneered, still holding Dale. "You think you're going to call the cops on me? A desperate bitch like you with your sniveling litter? Who else would have you?"

Nicky's hand moved quickly and quietly, lifting the knife from the dish rack. I don't think Phil noticed.

"I'm sorry, Phil," Mom said, remaining calm. "I didn't mean it. Let's go to bed. We can sort it out in the morning." She pushed David toward me with one hand. I grabbed him and shoved him behind me, into the kitchen.

Mom stepped towards Phil and Dale, nudging Fanny out of the way. She had to diffuse the situation before it got any more dangerous. She caught my eye. I knew she was counting on me to take care of the boys, get them to safety down the road, once she convinced Phil to join her back in bed.

Then, as if changing her mind, she suddenly stepped past Phil, heading toward Grandpa's room.

"What are you doing?" Phil shouted.

Mom didn't answer. She didn't have to. I knew what she was up to.

Grandpa always said a weapon was only as good as the person holding it. He didn't own a gun. He always said a determined criminal could overpower an honest man every time. A lethal weapon like a gun could be taken and used against you.

That didn't mean we shouldn't defend ourselves.

Nicky stepped past David and stood beside me, holding the large kitchen knife. For a second I thought he meant to pass it to me. After all, I was bigger and stronger.

When it came right down to it, though, he was probably tougher than I was. Squaring his shoulders, he prepared for battle.

"You've got to be kidding," Phil said. He looked at the knife in Nicky's hand. Holding Dale in front of him, he said, "I could snap your brother's neck like a twig. Is that what you want?"

"Nicky," I said, "give me the knife."

Reluctantly Nicky stepped back, handing me the weapon.

"That's more like it," Phil said. "Now, you boys get on the floor. Face down, side by side."

Nicky and I stood together, neither of us moving. I could hear David whimpering behind us, but I couldn't take my eyes off Phil long enough to check on him.

Nicky saw Mom come out of Grandpa's bedroom. When he realized what she meant to do, I could feel his energy change.

She had the advantage of surprise. With Phil focused on Nicky, me and the knife, she was able to bring up the rear.

She moved swiftly, leaving no chance for Phil to react.

In her hands was the only weapon Grandpa would allow in his house – the 1938 *Louisville Slugger*, the very one his father had given him. The same one he used when he taught me and Nicky to play ball on those long sun-filled days at his cottage, when he would be the father we never had, laughing and playing until we'd used up the last of his youthful vigor.

Phil never saw it coming.

One strike and he was out.

I ran for Dale, lifting him out of reach of the man we now knew to be a monster.

Phil groaned softly, stirring on the floor.

"Damn," Mom said.

"I can tie him up," I said.

"To hell with that."

She raised the bat once more, with steady surety, pausing for only an instant before bringing down the fatal blow.

Spent, she fell onto the couch. I think she was in shock. Her robe hung loosely, and she shivered. Her face was deadly white.

"Are you all right?" I asked.

Nicky brought a blanket from our room and covered her. I lifted her feet onto the couch.

"I'll be OK," she said. "Just give me a moment."

"We have to get him out of here," Nicky said, nodding at the bleeding mass that had been Phil.

I tried to take control of the situation, assuming my best television persona.

"I'll check his pulse," I said.

"Don't bother," Mom said, sitting up. "He's finished."

I thought she was probably right. His eyes were open, glazed over, staring blindly at the overhead fan.

"Give me the bat," Nicky said. "I'll clean it up."

"Good thinking," I said.

"I'll get dressed," Mom said.

"Me too. We can take him down to the dock."

"We have to take him further than that," she said. "We can use Grandpa's boat."

"I'll get the plastic tarp from the shed." My grandfather kept a couple of tarps, the kind you can tie to four trees to make an awning. We liked to sit under them when it rained, listening to the drops above our heads, all the while cheating nature by remaining outdoors and dry.

"There are rubber boots in the basement. Bring a pair for both of us."

"OK."

She headed for the master bedroom to get changed.

On my way to the stairs, I peeked into the bathroom. Nicky was doing a good job of cleaning the bat.

"I'm going to help Mom get rid of him," I said.

Nicky nodded.

"We'll leave Fanny with you and the boys. Can you clean the floor while we're gone?"

He nodded again.

"We can't leave any blood stains on the wood."

He knew what I meant. We both watched a lot of television.

"I'll move the furniture and make sure I get it all."

"Good. You'd better throw Mom's nightgown and robe into the washer. Dale and Fanny might need cleaning up, too. We'll try not to be too long."

"There's a deep spot over near where Mr. Branson likes to fish," Nicky said. "No one swims out that way."

"I know the spot."

"And John," he said, still scouring the bat, "make sure he stays down."

"I'll make sure."

In Grandpa's shed I found the wheelbarrow, some yellow nylon rope, a good, strong tarp and a cement block that had been broken in half.

I carried the tarp into the house. Nicky helped me roll Phil onto it. The floor under his head was still warm and slick. Then Nicky and Mom took one end of the tarp and I took the other, and together we carried him out to the yard.

We got both parts of the broken cement block into the tarp with Phil, then sealed it firmly with the heavy duty yellow rope before tipping the wheel barrow and rolling what was left of Phil into it. In the dark, we couldn't be sure we hadn't allowed any blood to escape, but we had no immediate neighbors. In the morning I'd come out and water the area, making sure to clean the wheel barrow.

"Boys, you mind Nicky while we're gone," Mom said to the twins. "Don't go into your room till you're clean."

They nodded.

I pushed the wheel barrow down to the dock. Phil was heavy, especially with the added weight of the cement block.

"That was good thinking," Mom said.

"Thanks."

She helped me get him into Grandpa's boat.

"I'll row," she said.

I was already bigger than she was, but I could tell her nerves were shot, so I didn't argue. Rowing gave her something to do.

We didn't talk much, at least not that I recall. When we were about half way to Branson's fishing spot, she paused in her rowing and looked up at the sky.

"Nearly a full moon," she said, taking care not to raise her voice. Sound carries easily on the water.

I looked to where she was pointing.

"I think it's supposed to be tomorrow night," I said.

"Johnny, tell me the truth. Was Phil molesting Dale?"

I looked away, studying the black water.

"I think so," I said.

"Me, too."

We found the spot, or near enough to it, and taking care not to tip the boat, we managed to roll him up and over the ledge.

He made a loud splash. It was over in a second. There aren't many people up that way, and even if anyone was awake, a splashing sound isn't unusual when you live near a lake.

"Well, that's that," Mom said.

"He'll stay down," I said.

"Would you mind rowing back? I'm kind of tired."

She traded spots with me and closed her eyes, turning her pale face up to the moonlight. I'd always thought of her as beautiful, and she was only thirty-one, but in that moment I could see the onset of age – the roots of tiredness spreading in tiny lines around her eyes.

Her blonde hair shone a ghostly silver, and I imagined: *This is how she'll look as an old woman. This is how she'll be in those last years before she dies.*

The thought made me sad.

I got us back as quickly as I could. Nicky was a tough bugger, but I knew the twins would be inconsolable, needing their mother.

I don't remember the rest of the weekend really. Mom called Grandpa on Saturday morning, spilling the whole story. He reminded her to go over everything with bleach, and he talked to me and the boys, telling us to stay calm.

"Don't panic," he said. "Cool heads will always prevail. Make sure you get rid of his belongings."

We stayed till Sunday night. Mom didn't want to raise suspicion by heading home early. We didn't do much – stayed in the cottage, close to Mom.

The drive back was long and quiet. We didn't make any stops.

We were all different somehow after that night. We went about our business in the usual way, keeping our routines. But a secret like that wears you down. We looked at each other with more knowing eyes.

Grandpa died a few years later. I don't know how I would've endured my teens without him – what kind of man I'd have become without his steady influence.

Nicky was, if possible, even more sullen in the years that followed, although he was a big help to Mom and me with the twins. He didn't like to leave them on their own – ever vigilant, I suppose – so he stayed close to home in the evenings, especially after I started dating.

Mom reported that a new salesperson from the drug manufacturing company had started calling on the pharmacy where she worked. A chatty young woman by the name of Selina. She and Mom became friends.

According to Selina, the previous salesperson, Phil, had up and disappeared, leaving the company without notice.

When police came around to speak to his co-workers, it was revealed Phil had a questionable history. He'd been accused on two separate occasions of impropriety towards children. In both cases, the victims and their single mothers had recanted. Charges were dropped.

Most likely, he'd been able to silence his previous victims with threats.

Phil met the wrong single mother the day he hooked up with Bessie Fender.

And now, more than twenty years later, I look out over the gathered congregation. Nicky isn't there. He joined the forces after high school and, like my father, never came back.

Dale and David remained bachelors. They have a house not far from Mom's. Today they're sitting in the front pew, together as always, near my wife, Samantha, and our daughter Bessie.

"My mother," I began, "believed in the irrepressible power of love."

My eyes sting. I'm not sure I can finish the eulogy.

But I know I must, and so I reach down deep inside myself for the courage to say goodbye...

...to the strongest, most loving person I will ever know.

About the Author

Donna Carrick is the author of *The First Excellence* (winner of the 2011 Indie Book Event Award), *Gold And Fishes* and *The Noon God*. Her Crime Anthologies, *Sept-Îles and other places* and *Knowing Penelope*, have been met with reader acclaim.

Her story "Watermelon Weekend", featured in *Thirteen* (Carrick Publishing), was shortlisted for the prestigious Arthur Ellis Award, 2014.

Donna's novels have reached over 100,000 readers worldwide.

Visit Donna at her Website
www.donnacarrick.com
at www.carrickpublishing.com
or at her Amazon Author Page